Me and the End of the World

Me and the End of the World

William Corbin

Simon & Schuster Books for Young Readers
Published by Simon & Schuster
New York • London • Toronto • Sydney • Tokyo • Singapore

SIMON & SCHUSTER
BOOKS FOR YOUNG READERS
Simon & Schuster Building, Rockefeller Center
1230 Avenue of the Americas
New York, New York 10020

10 9 8 7 6 5 4 3 2 1

Library of Congress Cataloging-in-Publication Data
Corbin, William.
Me and the end of the world / by William Corbin. p. cm.
Summary: After reading in the newspaper that the world
will end May 1, 1928, fourteen-year-old Tim sets out
to accomplish four goals.
[1. Self-confidence—Fiction.]   I. Title.   PZ7.C7998Me   1991
[Fic]—dc20   90-23559   CIP

ISBN: 0-671-74223-X

For Rich and Frances Robb,
who helped remember

Contents

CHAPTER

1

Will It or Won't It?

BY THE MIDDLE of last December just about everybody
had heard the world would come to an end the first
day of May.

I was slow to catch on, not being much for reading
newspapers or listening to the radio. But about a week
before Thanksgiving not even I could miss the big
picture on the front page of the *Des Moines Register*
showing a mob of people making these white robe
outfits which they would put on when the fatal day
came. Then they were going to climb to the top of a
high hill in the northwestern corner of Iowa and meet
their Maker. Underneath the picture it said hundreds
were joining up every day, so it looked like there'd be
thousands from all over the place—Minnesota and
Nebraska and Missouri and South Dakota and no
telling where else.

They'd all be singing and praying like sixty, the
paper said, and it would be a real sight to see. The
idea was pretty scary but all the same I thought that if

it wasn't for the white robe I wouldn't mind going along, if I had a way to get there.

In the days that followed I got to wondering some if it was really going to happen, everything going along the way it was, about normal. I knew of course that God must be in charge of it, and if He didn't know what He was doing then nobody did. But then I got to thinking what a waste it all would be, getting me clear up past the age of thirteen, and the whole world up to the age of nineteen hundred and twenty-eight and then—*whop*—chop 'er off!

When I asked my father if *he* thought the world was coming to an end, he said as far as he was concerned it already did, the first week of October when the Pirates lost the World Series to the Yankees four games straight. My father isn't especially a Pittsburgh fan, but he really hates the Yankees. My grandfather put in his two cents worth then and said my father was right for the wrong reason, the end having really come when Cal Coolidge announced he didn't choose to run again in 1928. And *that*, Grampa said, meant that as sure as God made little green apples we'd end up with Al Smith in the White House, so we might as well elect the Pope and be done with it.

Grampa didn't really live with us because most of the time he was out on the road selling for a dental supply company. His territory covered the whole state and slopped over into Omaha and southern Minnesota. He came mostly around holiday times, being a widower and having no other home to go to except for a little apartment just north of downtown which he said was barely big enough for him and two rats. I always enjoyed hearing him talk about the good old days, and he was never stingy about sharing his opinions on any subject that came up.

Anyway, I got the idea that neither he nor my father was losing much sleep over the end of the world, and I felt a little easier in my mind. But then I asked my mother, who looked sad and worried and said she hadn't wanted to mention it, me having such tender years, but that the pastor of our church, whose name is Reverend Pennywhistle, had come down hard on the side of the end-of-the-worlders and said his wife was already making robes for both of them. And that was good enough for my mother, him being a fine minister and nobody's fool.

Her sister, who is my aunt Lizzie, got in her licks too and said the way she looked at it, it was high time the world did come to an end, what with all the evil in it—young women putting paint on their faces and smoking cigarettes and dancing the night away and drinking gin right along with the men in those dreadful speakeasy places, and wearing their skirts clear up to—

"Lizzie!" my mother said, talking louder to drown her out. "I know you think you're being funny, but I don't care for the timing of it."

Aunt Lizzie said, "Oh, you mean little pitchers have big ears?"

My mother didn't answer, just rolled her eyes up toward the ceiling to show what a lot she had to put up with. The two of them don't see eye-to-eye about a lot of things and my aunt, who teaches math in high school and rents our big front room with the dormer window in it, is pretty sharp and is always needling my mother for being sort of straitlaced and stuffy. Me, I try not to get caught in the middle.

Anyway, I happened to know that my mother thought those things were pretty evil, all right. Maybe she was right, but what I wondered was, were they evil enough to call for shutting down the whole *world*?

For an opinion on that I managed to buttonhole my mother's younger brother, my uncle Art Kenworthy who also boards at our house and is known as a live wire and a go-getter. At only twenty-six years of age he is already manager of the National Cigar Store on Locust Street in the middle of downtown Des Moines. I figured he'd be pretty well informed on the subject of evil because he smokes cigars—ten-centers at that—and makes no bones about taking an occasional shot of bootleg hooch, and it wouldn't surprise me much to find out that he now and then helps one of those young women dance the night away.

Not only that, during baseball season he's in charge of the big scoreboard that covers the top half of a wall in the back room of the cigar store where a kid maybe sixteen or so chalks up the scores in big numbers as they come in over the radio. Before radio broadcasting got to the point where it is now, he even taught himself telegraphy so he could keep the scores coming when the regular telegrapher was off sick or drunk or something. Naturally they only keep score on the big league games, not the Des Moines Demons, which is in the Western League, and if you want to keep track of them you just jump on the streetcar and head for the ballpark.

Anyway, when I knocked on his door a while after

dinner (I'd have been there sooner but I have to dry dishes) he called out, "If that's you, Tim, come on in; anybody else needs an appointment." He's the only one calls me Tim. Everybody else says Timmie unless they're mad at me in which case it's Timothy. Or Timothy Andrew Walden.

He was dressing to go out, which wasn't what you'd call unusual. Putting a fresh collar on a shirt—and for once he didn't drop the stud so as I'd have to scramble around and find it for him. It was one of those new soft collars, not one of the hard-starched kind, and looked pretty spiffy once he'd put his tie on. Red with black polka dots. He can tie a bow tie faster than I can tie my shoelace and ten times neater.

"What's on your mind, sport?" he said. "You got five minutes to tell all."

So I got right down to it. Asked him his views about the world coming to an end. By the time I got through he had one foot up on a bench and was giving a shoe a good buffing with a brush. He finished that one, did the other one, then straightened up, looking about seven feet tall (he's really six feet two), and he said, "You really worried about this?"

I said I wouldn't call it worried, more like just a little uneasy. He thought about that awhile and said, "That makes two of us. Tell you what we'll do, you and me. Come May Day—day before, rather—we'll jump in the old flivver and mosey up there to the big doin's. Way I figure, if it's going to happen, we'll be better off hanging around with the folks doing all the praying. If it turns out the other way, we'll go fishing. Some good lakes up there, and we might come back with a mess of bass. How's that strike you?"

Well, it was the best proposition I could remember, but before I could say so I got nagged by a thought that took the shine out of the day and I said, "Wouldn't be right, would it, to go without Mother and Dad? You know—at a time like that."

Before I'd even got all the words out he was shaking his head. Then he grabbed his pants off the back of a chair and got into them, buttoning up quick, the way he does everything. "Wouldn't work at all," he said. "Your mother hates fishing and your dad can't stand praying."

That made sense and I said so, but right away I got nagged again. "We have to get rigged out in those white robes?"

He pulled his suspenders over his shoulders and let them snap and reached for his coat and vest. "Take along a couple bedsheets and nobody'll notice. It's not the style that counts, it's the principle."

He got out a handkerchief and arranged it in the breast pocket so that all four corners showed. Really nifty. "It's all settled then," he said. "Just you and me, and we don't need to tell anyone till the time comes." He sort of shrugged so the coat would settle down on his shoulders just so. "How do I look?" he said.

"Not as good as you would in a bedsheet," I said, and ducked when he took a swing at me.

"Anything I can't stand it's a smart-aleck kid," he said, and with that went down the stairs with a racket like a team of horses.

Well, I guess it's easy to see why I always wish my mother would ease up on him, quit going on about how he ought to stop living so wild and settle down and raise a family. I suppose he will some day, but I wish she wouldn't rush him so. It would mean he wouldn't live with us anymore, and I don't know how I could do without him.

My dad comes right out and says, "Leave him alone, Nell. His weekly contribution comes in real handy. Why nag him into getting hitched and handing it over to some flapper we never even met?" Smart as he is, being an insurance company executive, you'd think my father would have learned by now she doesn't think teasing is funny. Not when it's about serious things.

Anyway, I felt a lot easier in my mind after talking to Uncle Art, but there was still one person left to check in with: Miss Wilson, my English teacher, that being my best subject. She's real tall for a lady, kind of awkward in the way she moves, and it's a safe bet she never had anybody like Uncle Art hanging around her when she was young. You'd have to say she's mostly homely except for her eyes, which are dark and deep-set with a way of sort of glowing at you when you come up with an answer that pleases her. They can also do a blowtorch job on you if you've been doing less than your best. Some of the kids say she scares them, some say they hate her. Far as I'm concerned, I'll go for the glow anytime and leave the blowtorch for somebody else.

It took a little organizing—like managing the next day to accidentally pass the door to Miss Wilson's room right after school and finding her still at her desk. I walked right in before I could lose my nerve and apologized for interrupting and asked if she would mind a question.

She put down the papers in her hand and smiled

with her eyes. (You've got to look close to see it.) And she said, "Anytime, Timmie."

So I fired away. "Do you believe what everybody's saying, that the world is coming to an end next May Day?"

She looked at me pretty close while she thought about it, and finally she said, "No, I don't believe it—but on the other hand I don't believe in saying a thing *can't* happen. In my time, Timmie, many things have happened that I would once have said were impossible. So now I believe that *anything* can happen."

Right away then she looked at me in kind of a considering way—the way you would if you were guessing how much somebody weighed—and she banged a question right back at me. "Tell me," she said. "If you knew—or really *believed*—this thing would happen, what would you do? I mean, what would you do that you wouldn't do otherwise?"

Well, for a second I wished I'd gone straight home. Nobody had ever asked me a question before that started tipping me straight over the edge of a cliff that had no bottom to it. In another second, though, I knew the answer and I said, "I wouldn't do anything different, I guess. I'd just do it faster." There were a lot of things I wanted to do but I wasn't counting on having to *hurry*.

Miss Wilson picked up a pencil and rolled it between her fingers, forwards, backwards, watching the pencil, not me, and she said, "Could you give me a few examples?"

Until she asked that I'd have said an answer would be easy, but now I couldn't begin to think fast enough to get a grip on all the fragments of ideas that went pinwheeling through my head.

Having no answer for something as important as this made me feel like a real lunkhead and I had to say, "Gee, Miss Wilson, I just flat out don't know. If I had time to think a little, I'd—"

"Take time," she said. "This is interesting, and I'd very much like to know your answer. Let's see now." She tapped the desk a few times with her pencil. "This is Friday. Think about it over the weekend—write things down if you'd like—and come back after school on Monday."

I must have let a noticeable time go by before I said I'd do it, because she gave me a reassuring sort of smile. "Don't leave anything out because you think it might seem silly, or too personal, or anything of the sort. I promise absolute confidentiality. If anybody lets the cat out of the bag it won't be me."

I stumbled all over myself telling her how sure I was she'd never even think of spilling the beans about whatever I might tell her. Then I said good-bye and thanks and headed for home.

I turned all the right corners and crossed all the right streets without getting run over, but it wasn't because I was paying attention to where I was going. I wasn't well enough organized to line up a set of answers for Miss Wilson on Monday. Instead I kept worrying about what I'd got myself into. Maybe the whole thing was pointless. Counting Grampa, I'd got five opinions, and only my mother's was solidly on the side of the world-enders. All the others—including Miss Wilson—were various degrees of doubtful.

If I threw in the views of Ed Guthrie, my best

friend, who was the first person I'd ever talked to about it, I'd have a positive *no* vote to balance against my mother's *yes*. Ed called it a lot of bushwah, horsefeathers, and things like that. So it all added up to a pretty weak case for the end of the world and maybe I oughtn't to let the idea bother me so. On the other hand, if I could talk to twenty people, or a hundred, I'd likely get another answer altogether. I went around and around like that even after I'd made it home and tried calming myself down with a couple of peanut butter sandwiches. If only something would happen that would put me firmly on one side or the other!

Something did, and Ed Guthrie was responsible for it.

Ed and I have been best friends all our lives—probably since the first time our mothers wheeled us side by side in our baby carriages. We were born a week apart, me in my house on Thirty-fifth Street and Ed in his, right around the corner on School Street. Since then there can't have been very many days we haven't spent some time together, riding everything from kiddie kars and little red wagons on up to bikes and roller coasters. About the only thing we've never done together—hard to believe—is go to school. The reason for that is that the line between two school districts runs right between our houses, and neither district would give an inch when our folks tried to get one or the other of us transferred. My mother is fond of quoting somebody on the school board as saying, "It can't be did!"

Anyway, Ed was responsible, because it was his idea that we were in the front row at the Orpheum Theater

Saturday afternoon having the pants scared off us by Lon Chaney in *The Phantom of the Opera*. It was also Ed's fault that we'd got to the theater a few minutes late and missed the short subjects that come before the movie. This meant we'd have to see the movie, then the vaudeville show, then stay to see the short subjects because we never could stand missing anything we'd paid a dime apiece to see. Especially this time, because I'd read in the paper that the newsreel was being shown with this new sound process so you could *hear* what the announcer was saying instead of just reading words on the screen. I couldn't believe it at first but then the paper went on to say that the process was being perfected so that in only a year or two everything, movies and all, would come with sound. Anyway, Ed and I knew this was sure something we didn't want to miss.

Well, as they say, we didn't know the half of it. The Phantom gave us plenty of chills and thrills just as promised by the posters out front, but to my way of thinking it was about as chilling and thrilling as *Little Lord Fauntleroy* compared with what happened when the short subjects rolled around.

The newsreel came first, starting with a big fanfare of trumpets that could have knocked your hat off. The whole theater let out a gasp and the announcer's face filled up the screen with the credits appearing behind him. His voice was deep and powerful in spite of scratchiness you could tell came from the sound machinery rather than from him.

"We are about to show you," he said, "a scene that is being viewed in varying forms throughout the length and breadth of the land. Everywhere our fellow citizens in countless numbers are joining a movement that foretells the world's end on the coming first day of May."

While he talked the camera moved to this big hill near the ocean in California. The spooky thing was that I recognized the place. It was the hill I'd seen in the paper a couple of weeks before when there was nothing on it but a crane and a bunch of workmen putting a huge cross in place.

The cross was standing free now, towering over the hilltop which was thick with people—hundreds and hundreds of them—all looking toward a huge pulpit at the base of the cross. Room enough for about a dozen preachers, it looked like, but there was only one in it now. Behind the pulpit, apparently fastened to the upright shaft of the cross, was a huge figure of an angel—twenty feet high, maybe—made out of wood or plaster and painted with something that shone like gold in the sun. The angel held a trumpet to its mouth with one hand while the other was stretched out toward the people, sort of beckoning.

The camera moved slowly closer, and the angel got taller and taller and mightier and mightier, until a chill went rippling up my back. Ed shifted around in the seat beside me and said in a whisper, "Holy smoke —why are all those people there *now*? They in a hurry?"

I'd been wondering the same thing, but in a few moments I knew, because the camera moved down to the figure of that lone preacher, who had white hair and a robe to match. As his figure filled the screen he raised both arms, and as if on a signal the announcer shut up and here came the preacher's voice, thunderous and solemn: "It's not too late, good friends. That's why we are here today. It is never too late to accept, to believe, to take shelter in the loving shadow of the Almighty!"

He paused, and in the hush an organ began to play—one of those portable pump organs like they have at Y camp. A feeble little sound, considering the surroundings, but it could be heard, and everybody knows the hymn. Now the preacher started beating time to the music and thundered out: "*Everybody now*—and put your *souls* into it!" They did: "*Mine eyes have seen the glo-ry of the coming of the Lord. . . .*"

Then a lone voice from one of the back rows in the theater joined in: ". . . *He is trampling out the vintage where the grapes of wrath are stored. . . .*" And in no time at all the lone voice was joined by more and more until the whole theater seemed ready to burst with the sound of it. Well, that hymn always has given me a case of the spine-ripples, but never like this time, with all that mob of people on the screen gathered on purpose to get *ready* for the coming of the Lord, and no telling how many right there in the theater cocked and primed to join them on the spur of the moment. It was grand and overpowering and scary.

The singing only lasted as long as the first glory glory hallelujah, and then the scene faded from the screen and there was the announcer again, and pretty soon he was finished and it was time for the Our Gang comedy. I was ready to laugh at anything at all to take my mind off what I'd been seeing and hearing.

I did forget it, but never for long. They kept coming

back, those sights and sounds, as if I'd been running the newsreel over and over just for myself. I didn't get any comfort out of it.

What I did get was scared. The trouble with a good imagination is that it keeps improving on reality. Without trying to or wanting to I'd find myself up on that hill with the prayerful uproar all around, straining my eyes toward the first faint light in the eastern sky. Waiting. Waiting for a monstrous explosion of sound like the roar of a thousand volcanoes and a blinding burst of light like the blaze of a million suns.

That was one way. Another was the end, in a single eyewink, of all sound and movement except for birds plunging from the sky, people dropping where they stood. How much of it would I see, or hear? How long a time would I have to be afraid in?

It was hard to say what I really believed would happen, but that newsreel had done what no amount of reading or arguing or thinking could have done. That crowd of people on the hill in California, the words of the preacher, and the way they all lit into "mine eyes have seen the glory," joined on the spur of the moment by maybe half the people in the Orpheum Theater, convinced me that the sensible thing to do was take the whole thing as seriously as they did.

Even Ed Guthrie was impressed by what we'd seen and heard. I could tell, even though he wouldn't admit it and started pooh-poohing it all right afterwards. "Just because a lot of people—or even *every-body*—believes something," he argued, "doesn't mean it's so. Everybody used to believe the earth was flat, didn't they? But nobody ever fell off the edge of it!"

He went on to say I'd got myself all worked up because of the preaching and praying and singing.

I said I wasn't worked up but there was no use arguing about something you felt was true right down to your bones.

To that he said, "Well, let me know how your bones feel about it when you wake up on the second of May and the birds are singing and you're there to listen to them."

I said if that happened I'd be as glad as anybody, and we left it at that. Maybe it would turn out that way, I thought. But until it did I wasn't going to take any chances. If the end of the world was coming I wanted to be as ready for it as I could get. If it wasn't, I wouldn't have lost anything but a little time and a lot of effort. What I needed right now was some serious thinking about what to tell Miss Wilson on Monday.

2

Plan of Action

I SPENT MOST of Sunday thinking about it. Homework, I called it when my mother asked, but it was about ten times harder than any real homework. I kept my Latin book open on my desk just in case, and I probably looked like a hard-working student, but what I was actually doing was breaking my brain over what I really wanted to accomplish before the world shut down.

It didn't take long to realize I didn't have time to do a tenth—maybe a hundredth—of the things that occurred to me. I'd need four *years*, not just four months. I made a list. Scratched out about two-thirds of it. Added a few. Wadded the list up, threw it in the wastebasket. Chewed a pencil to splintery bits. Made another list, a lot shorter but not short enough. Into the wastebasket with that one too.

And so on. If I'd spent as much time studying my eighth-grade Latin as I did making those lists I'd have been fluent enough to talk Julius Caesar out of crossing the Rubicon. In the end it was an inspiration that told me what to do. There may have been a better way but I was running out of sanity, and anyway, inspirations don't come along in bunches, like celery. What mine told me was that the first three or four things I'd thought of—and written first—were likely the most important. To me, that is; never mind how they might look to anyone else.

So all right—do or die—full speed ahead. I scrabbled in the wastebasket and came up with the messy ball of paper with my first list on it. Feeling sort of tensed-up, as if this was the map of where the treasure was buried—or the bodies—I smoothed it out and reread what fate had in mind for the rest of my life. It looked, with the messed-up parts corrected—like this:

1. Fight Dunk Bolander.
2. Apologize to Mr. Weinstock.
3. Hitch rides on my sled along that route I keep thinking about.
4. Kiss Judy Felton.

After that came a bunch of scratched-out items. I didn't even try to read them and didn't look any farther. Using my ruler I tore off the first four and crammed the rest back into the wastebasket. Talk about the Rubicon!

I got out a new sheet of paper and used a pen to copy the four items in my best printing—my best handwriting is none too good. I read it over again and had to admit that to anyone but me it sure wouldn't look like much. Why would anybody think that puny little collection of oddments just *had* to be done before I got wiped out along with the rest of the human race? But so what? Nobody but me had been promising himself to accomplish every one of these things.

Sooner or later. Some day. When I got around to it. But now there were only four months and a week left, and everything was different.

Nothing to do now but wait for tomorrow so I could show the list to Miss Wilson. In one way I wished I didn't have to go through with it for fear she'd think it was as dumb as I halfway thought myself. In another way I didn't care how dumb she thought it was, because I was going to do these things if the time allowed, no matter what anybody thought.

Same as on Friday, I waited till all the kids in her last class had left, then eased through the door. She was shuffling through papers, putting some in drawers, others in her satchel to take home. Catching sight of me she studied my face as thoroughly as if the police had asked her for a description. Then she nodded, with one of her near-smiles, as if I'd given the right answer to a question. "Done your homework, have you?"

"Yes ma'am," I said, taking the list from my shirt pocket and unfolding it. "Got a list here." Handed it over. "It doesn't look like much, but it really is."

"I wouldn't doubt it for a moment." She flattened out the paper on her desk and read it while I squirmed. It seemed to take a long time before she looked up. "Unless it's *very* private," she said, "would you fill in a few details?"

I said, "Oh sure. I expected to."

She looked back at the list. "To begin, who is Dunk Bolander?"

"Fellow I know down at the Y," I told her.

"And fighting him is important enough to go at the head of your list?"

"I didn't plan it that way," I said, "but—yes—it is."

She looked doubtful but nodded anyway. "Better make sure you can win it then."

I didn't blame her for doubting it, having no way of knowing what was behind it. "I'd tell you about it," I said, "but it's a long story."

"That's the trouble with a lot of stories. Very well, what about Mr. Weinstock?"

Just thinking about me and Mr. Weinstock made me cringe inside. Maybe outside too. But I had to say something, so I said, "Well, he'd . . . it's . . ."

Her eyes crinkled up. "Another long story?"

"Too long," I said, "and too awful." It occurred to me she wasn't really getting much out of this conversation and I tried to do better. "He's our next-door neighbor," I said. "Real nice man and, well, I decided I couldn't stand it if the world was to end and I'd never told him I was sorry for . . . for what I did."

She rubbed her pencil along the side of her nose for a few seconds, still looking down at my list, then suddenly she peered straight up at me. "Timmie, I've got an idea! Who knows, it might even be a good one."

"Yes, ma'am?"

"Write it down!"

I must have looked as blank as I felt and she hurried to explain. "For most of us it's easier to write than to talk when we feel strongly about something. Why don't you explain these things to me in writing? You're a reader, you write well, so it shouldn't be hard for you to do. Between now and the first of May keep a record of what you do to make your list work out, and why you do it. Call it an assignment—and maybe we'll both learn something."

Miss Wilson is a hard person to say *no* to. Maybe I didn't even want to. I said I guessed I could make a stab at it. She said, "Bully for you!" and fired another question. "I have an awful feeling I can guess, but would you please explain a little about this 'hitching rides'?"

That was one subject I had no objection to talking about, seeing it was probably my favorite winter sport. "First you need lots of snow. Then you get in position behind a car that's about to start off," I said. "Get down on your sled and grab hold of the rear bumper with one hand, hang on to your sled with the other. You stay with it as long as it's going the way you want to go, then let go and grab a ride on another car. If you've got a definite route in mind, the way I said on my list, you have to make a lot of false starts and go to all kinds of trouble and keep to a time schedule too. It's not easy."

She said, "In other words, you get yourself dragged through busy streets behind cars driven by strangers who don't know you're there, through congested intersections, and all this on packed snow that's none too safe to begin with."

"Well, it'll be evening when I do it, not so much traffic then."

She half sighed, half snorted, and said, "Timmie, I can't imagine why you worry about the end of the world when you're not likely to live to see the day."

I told her it wasn't near as dangerous as it sound-ed—which wasn't really the strict truth, because I could remember a few times when I'd prayed I was home in bed instead of out on the frozen streets. But I try not to burden grown-ups with the strict truth when it might be an inconvenience to them. A happy thought struck me then and I added, "Besides, I always go with my best friend, Ed. He and I look out for each other. And I can truthfully say we're experts."

"And I suppose you can truthfully say your parents applaud this, er, form of recreation?"

I must have looked scared she might consider it her duty to talk to them about it, but she sighed again, real deeply this time, and said, "God forgive me, but I must respect a confidence!" She looked at the list again. "And now for the last." She thought for a second or two and spoke to herself. "Felton, Judy. Copper hair? Green eyes? Lots of sparkle?"

I was starting to squirm a little because of the subject matter, and she must have noticed. "No need to comment on this one. It's, er, self-explanatory."

I said, "I guess you think it's pretty dopey to put a thing like that on a list as important as this, but—"

She interrupted. "I already think you might get killed. Is dopey worse than dead?"

"Maybe not," I said, "but managing to do that is a lot scarier than hitching rides."

She crinkled up again. "I've yet to hear of a kiss putting anyone in the hospital."

I said there was always a first time and she laughed, then started picking up her papers, bumping their edges to get them straight, so I figured I'd used up all the time I was entitled to. I thanked her and started out.

I'd made it to the door when she stopped me. "Hold on, Timmy!" She put the papers and a book or two into the satchel thing she carried and stood up. "I just want you to know I'm *honored* to be in your confidence.

Your, er, private concerns will be safe with me. See you tomorrow."

Well—wow! I'd never *honored* anybody before, least of all a teacher—a teacher like Miss Wilson. It wasn't the sort of thing you could go around bragging about: "Hey, look at me—I make people feel *honored*." But it was a thing you could enjoy all by yourself, going over and over the words, like a private phonograph record, and feeling satisfied and warm and sort of *worthy*.

What I didn't know was that a thing like that could show. When I walked in the front door there was my sister, Felice, standing in the middle of the room flipping through the afternoon mail which she'd just got out of the box by the door. Being nearly two years older and in high school, she usually did her best to ignore me, but this time she gave me what started out as a glance but turned into a sharpish look and said, "What's up with you? They just elected you the kid most likely to succeed?" She's got an eye like an eagle's and if you've got any secrets you'd better be sure to wear a deadpan when she's around. I guess it goes with being an artist and always drawing anybody who holds still long enough to take a deep breath.

I told her I didn't know what she was talking about and couldn't a person think a pleasant thought now and then without attracting a lot of attention.

Instead of coming back at me with something sharp she flashed what I have to admit is a million-dollar smile and said, "Maybe you're not the only one who can enjoy a few pleasant thoughts."

Well, I wasn't about to swap secrets with her, but I

knew an invitation when it hit me in the eye, so I said, "I didn't get elected anything, but I bet *you* did."

"Well, sort of," she said, trying to look modest—not the easiest thing in the world for her. "I was the only sophomore chosen to submit a cover design for the new yearbook. Only others in the running are a junior and two seniors!"

"Wow—nice going!" I said. "I hope you come out on top."

She smiled again. With eyes almost as dark as her hair and a set of teeth fit for a toothpaste ad, she rates a second look from guys with their eyes open. She said, "You know—I just might!" She sashayed over to the foot of the stairs, put the mail on the little table, and called, "Mother—you up there?"

The news was about to spread, I figured. Whatever it was she'd seen in my face was already forgotten, which suited me fine except that it would have been nice to be asked about it.

I went to the kitchen and made myself a couple of slices of cinnamon toast. While I chomped away on it I started thinking again along the lines I wished weren't getting to be such a habit with me. It wouldn't be much of a surprise, I thought, if Felice's design was chosen for the yearbook cover. But would there *be* a yearbook for 1928? Did she think about things like that, and if she did would she talk to *me* about it?

I cleaned up after myself and went up to my room to start figuring out how to go about starting on the list of things I had to do before May Day—*and* how to write about it for Miss Wilson. It's not easy for anyone, even me, to understand how so short and simple a list of projects could look as tough as digging the Panama Canal with a shovel.

Apologizing to Mr. Weinstock, for example. Sure, it would only take about five minutes, but it would also take more guts than I probably had. There couldn't be anything easy about taking the blame for doing something so low and rotten that just the thought of it makes your toes curl and your scalp get hot.

The next item on the list—hitching rides—was the only one that could possibly be easy, but even that would take a lot of plain fool luck, plus more cooperation from the weather than I had any right to expect.

Kissing Judy Felton. I'd been wanting to do that for so long I couldn't stand the idea that the world would end and I'd never even *tried*. So there it was on my list and at this point my chances of doing it looked about on a level with my chance of kissing Clara Bow, the movie star. The difference was I didn't want to kiss Clara Bow.

In any case, however hard it might be to actually kiss Judy, there wouldn't be any pain connected with it. Far from it! But when it came to Dunk Bolander I couldn't imagine anything *but* pain. Just thinking about it gave me that falling-elevator feeling in the pit of my stomach.

Dunk Bolander is a guy about my age and height but heavier. Muscle, not fat, worse luck.

I'd never even heard of him until about three weeks before, when he showed up one day at the YMCA where I go a lot to swim and play games. I found out he lives in what's considered a tough area on the north side of town, and he makes a point of living up to that reputation. Black hair, heavy black eyebrows that he sort of lowers over squinted eyes in order to look dangerous. As far as I'm concerned, it works. He keeps his thumbs hooked under his belt a lot and is always hunching his shoulders like gangsters' bodyguards in movies, and when he's outside he spits a lot from between his teeth.

I decided pretty quick that he was a guy I could get along with fine as long as we didn't have anything to do with each other. He didn't leave it that way though. One afternoon around Thanksgiving I was playing pingpong when he came in. He started watching the game which was going hot and heavy. It's not bragging to say I'm pretty good at pingpong, having won the tournament for my age group at Y camp.

After a while he said, "I'll take on the winner."

The winner turned out to be me, so he and I started in and it didn't take long to know that he was good but I was better. I beat him two games in a row and he slammed his paddle down on the table and said, "I never played no left-hander before. Threw me off my game."

I said, "Well, if I played with my right hand it would sure throw *my* game off."

He let me have that slitty-eyed look and said, "Don't get smart with me, Bo!" Bo is what you call people to show you're tough. Maybe if I'd done something right then—something to show I was a little bit tough myself—things might have turned out differently. But I didn't.

The first thing happened about an hour later. The swimming lesson was over and we had fifteen minutes to just horse around in the pool. I was standing on the edge deciding whether to dive under or over somebody when a hand shoved me in the middle of the back—hard—and in I went. When I surfaced I saw Dunk Bolander standing up there watching me with a phony grin. I grinned back, pretending to be a good sport. And after all, who hasn't pushed somebody into the water one time or another? But I didn't feel good about it. From then on I kept an eye out for him and if I saw him coming my way I'd dive in before he got close, as if I was planning to do it anyway. I didn't feel good about that, either. There just isn't any way to feel good about letting somebody pick on you because you're scared of him. And now that I'd seen him with his clothes off, that's what I was—scared. He looked like he had a black eye for me in either hand.

Ever since then he'd thought up other ways to get at me. In the shower once, after swimming, when I was all soaped up and couldn't open my eyes he flipped my lever over to cold and nearly gave me heart failure. I couldn't see him do it, but I heard him haw-hawing. Once he claimed he was ahead of me in the line waiting to use the diving board, which we both knew he wasn't, and I let him get away with it. Another time I was halfway home when I discovered a big wad of gum stuck inside my cap, and therefore in my hair. One guess was enough to know who put it there.

I can't remember which thing was one too many. All I know is that at some point I came to a decision: Either I'd go on hating myself for the rest of my life or I'd fight this guy. Win or lose—and I'd probably lose—I'd have done it and could live with myself. I made the decision back when I thought I had all the time in the world. Now, of course, there was hardly any time at all.

I spent an hour explaining about Dunk Bolander on paper, for Miss Wilson. Writing it all down had the effect of making the whole thing realer, the time shorter, and my predicament more desperate. What I'd planned, back when time didn't matter, was to take boxing lessons there at the Y. By the time I'd finished the beginners' course I'd probably have enough confidence to go on to the advanced course where I could find somebody to spar around with after the class was over, improving all the time, and waiting for the right moment for the big showdown.

Good plan then. Lousy now. Ready or not, I'd have to stick up for myself.

The time was past for mooning around trying to decide if the world was or wasn't going to end. Time now to get things *moving*, and the place to start was the boxing class. I'd go down to the Y tomorrow after school, find out the schedule, and sign up for the course.

CHAPTER

3

Sign Here for Punishment

THE FINAL BELL was still ringing in my ears next afternoon when I zipped out the Crocker Street side of the building and hightailed it to the streetcar stop.

Riding the cars is usually restful. I can halfway doze and daydream and the time passes fast. Not this time. I couldn't even close my eyes, and any daydream I got started on ended in a hurry—with me getting knocked on my can. I got off and headed for the Y building about as eagerly as if the dentist would be waiting for me there. Then up the steps, through the recreation room, and down the hall beyond leading to the gym.

I was heading for Red Clifford's office which is a cubbyhole off the side of the gym where a bunch of older guys were playing a noisy game of basketball. Red is the athletic director and the favorite of everybody around there. Nothing ever goes on that he doesn't know about.

I found him hunched over the litter on his desk like a bear guarding a log full of honey. I thought of a bear because of his size and his usual getup, baggy gray sweatsuit with a big yellow Y on the front and a whistle dangling in front of it on a woven leather cord.

Nothing bearlike in his smile, though, when I came sidling through the door. His eyes slitted up in a twinkle, not especially because it was me; it was the way he looked at all the boys most of the time. "I'm sorry to bother you, Mr., er, Red," I began, "but I—"

"What I get paid for," he interrupted. "Bein' bothered by a collection of scruffy boys. What's on your mind?"

"Well sir . . ." I took a deep breath. No way to back out now. "I want to sign up for the next boxing class."

It wouldn't have surprised me if he'd busted out laughing but he just nodded. "Beginners' group?"

Well, what else? If it hadn't been Red I'd have thought I was getting the needle. I said, "Yessir," and he leaned back, stared up at the ceiling, and proceeded to prove that, however cluttered his office might be, his brain was neat. Out of all the jumble of events, schedules, dates, and facts he must have been responsible for, he plucked out, like jack-straws, all the bits of information I needed. "You're in luck. Current class ends Friday—day before Christmas Eve. Next one starts January seventh. One-thirty to three every Saturday in the gym, up to and including . . . um . . . the last Saturday in March. We furnish the gloves. No other special gear needed. Wear your regular gym togs. Here"—he scrabbled in a drawer and handed me a mimeographed form—"have a seat over there and fill it out. Here's a pen."

The form had spaces for name and address, weight, height, and a list of physical disabilities. I didn't have any of those, at least that I knew about, and in a minute I handed the form back. He put it in the middle of a small sheaf of forms and I wondered if it would ever be seen again. "You're all set." As I started to thank him again he interrupted, this time with a grin. "One more thing."

"Yessir?"

"Get ready to sweat. You don't sweat, you don't get much out of it."

He waved me on my way and I went out to the recreation room and got my basket from the guy at the front desk and went swimming. I can't say I didn't keep my eye out for Dunk Bolander. There was no sign of him so I figured he wasn't going to show up and went upstairs where I found a guy wanting to play a game of pingpong. We played two games, winning one apiece, and would have played another to break the tie but I suddenly looked at one of the big windows and saw it was starting to get dark. Past time to head for home. So I said something about giving the guy a raincheck, grabbed my jacket, and headed for the door like a scared rabbit.

The door opens onto the wide hallway that leads to the front entrance and divides the recreation room from the front office. I wheeled through the doorway, turning right at the same time, and—*wham!*—tripped over a leg suddenly flung out in front of me. I had about a tenth of a second to recognize the owner of the leg before my momentum took me staggering down and across the hall like a drunk just thrown out the saloon door.

Arms flailing, I stumbled along a diagonal line between the recreation room door and the door to the office. Now came that infuriating *haw-haw-haw* that I remembered all too well and I told myself I had to stay on my feet for only one reason: to go charging back and swing a fist at that mocking face, whatever might happen to me afterwards. But fortunately, or unfortunately, depending on the point of view, Fate had other plans for me.

At that moment the glass door to the office swung suddenly open and out came one of the young women who worked there. She was a large young woman, and because she was calling good night to somebody inside, she came out backwards and didn't know I even existed until I came crashing into her. We both uttered an *Oooph!* at the same time, but she got in a few real words first. Swinging around, she said, "Great Heavens, boy, you know better than to run in the hall. And why don't you look where you're going?"

I guess I didn't really whimper and whine, but that's what it felt like while I burbled things like "Oh, gee, ma'am, I'm awful sorry . . . hurry to catch streetcar . . . somebody tripped . . . gosh, hope I didn't hurt . . . sorry . . ."

After a few more mouthfuls of that kind of thing she suddenly smiled, looking real pretty, and said, "Oh, well, no harm done, I quess. After all, I *was* coming out the door *backward*. What do you say we both leave now—slowly and facing forward?"

I opened the heavy front door and held it for her while she went out. Last thing I did was turn and look back up the hall. The *haw-haw* had stopped at some point and there was no one to be seen.

Quick-stepping toward the streetcar stop, I kept playing the last ten minutes over in my mind and found I was actually getting satisfaction out of the fact that I could get mad enough to try tangling with Dunk Bolander. Of course, my nasty inner voice piped up with *Oh sure! Feels great so long as you don't have to do it!*

All the same, for the first time I was really looking forward to the day I'd put those boxing gloves on. Steer clear of that Tim Walden—he's a tiger!

I didn't come back to earth until I was almost to the streetcar stop and suddenly caught on that I was cold. There was a brisk wind that seemed to come from all directions, women were clutching their coats in front and men were turning the collars of their topcoats up. I didn't have anything to clutch or turn up so I buttoned the top button of my jacket and hoped my car would be along PDQ.

Right then I realized, surprised-like, that for quite a while my head had been so full of the end of the world and what I proposed to do about it that I'd hardly thought at all about the weather. Earlier, I'd hardly thought about anything else.

Reason for that was that Iowa seemed to be getting some other state's weather. Arkansas's, maybe. Even New Mexico's. Ordinarily we could count on snow anywhere from the first of November on, and by Christmastime some real cold. Now, here it was almost Christmas with no snow at all and hardly enough cold to freeze a birdbath, let alone a four- or five-inch layer of ice on the lakes and ponds. Winter without snow for sledding and ice for skating would be like summer without swimming and baseball. Worse, even. Especially because I'd written a letter to Santa Claus in care of Frank Walden, who is my father, and put it in our mailbox. It said what I wanted most for

Christmas was the pair of hockey skates featured in the window of Van Ginkel's Sporting Goods and that Mr. Van Ginkel would know which pair I was talking about. It said also that I was really getting sick of those old clamp-on skates, which could always be counted on to come unclamped and pitch me headfirst onto the ice just when I had the puck and a clear shot at the goal. I signed it, "Your good friend and admirer, Timothy Walden," and waited for somebody to mention it. When nobody did I figured the skates were as good as wrapped and under the tree. Otherwise somebody would have kidded me about it—Uncle Art if nobody else.

That was a while before Thanksgiving, but when a month went by and still no snow and ice, I began to think there never would be. Now, in the nearly two hours I'd been in the Y building the temperature had dropped and the wind come up. Maybe something was on the way from Canada via North Dakota that would make Iowa act like its normal self.

The streetcar felt a lot warmer than it probably was and I managed to get all the way to my stop without giving a thought to the end of the world.

I was concentrating on how this very streetcar would take me right to the edge of Waveland Park, where there was a fair-sized pond you could get to on foot. It was actually the water hole of Waveland Golf Course and sometimes in the summer Ed and I would go out there and dredge up balls that hadn't made it across. We did it by taking our shoes and socks off, rolling our pant legs up, and walking around on the muddy bottom until we felt a ball. We'd get pretty wet reaching down to pick it up, but once we'd collected all we could hold in our hands and pockets we'd take them up to the pro shop and get anywhere from a nickel for two to a quarter for three, depending on the condition of the balls.

In the winter, once the city parks department had declared the ice safe for skating, it would look like a different place altogether. In really cold weather, getting down toward zero, the city would truck in firewood, set up benches in a circle, and keep a fire going on weekends and holidays. The benches would be full of people putting on their skates or taking them off. Some even brought weenies and buns and made hot dogs, so that if you weren't hungry already you soon would be from smelling the wood smoke and the toasting weenies dripping into the coals.

I got off the streetcar into the teeth of a north wind that felt like it had been making noses run in Saskatchewan at breakfast time, and I'd hardly gone a hundred feet up the slope toward home when another old friend put in an appearance: *snow*. It was almost too fine to see, especially with dusk coming on fast, but first it tickled, then it stung my face and ears and made me squeeze my eyes to slits for protection.

Under my breath I whooped "hot zigetty spit!" and other enthusiastic expressions. I reminded myself that this could easily be a false alarm with nothing useful coming out of it, but the odds were certainly on my side. After all, it was Iowa and January was right around the corner. I encouraged myself to go on daydreaming about the Waveland Park pond, me on my new skates, the envy of one and all.

If this snow would just keep coming long enough, it wouldn't be long before Ed and I would be out with our sleds. If it was going to be our last chance ever, we'd darn well better make the most of it.

By the time I got home the snow was blowing sideways on the streets and sidewalks but whitening and clinging in the winter-bleached grass of the lawns and making rooftop pencil lines along the valleys where one slope of roof met another. It was so dry it struck the bare trees with a constant hissing sound that raised my hopes another notch because dry snow, while it won't pile up fast, won't start to melt the minute the sun comes up.

As always I went in the side door which opens on a landing that's eight steps up from the basement and four steps down from the first floor and has a row of hooks for outdoor clothes. I hung up my stuff and went up. The second I opened the door to the little hall that goes from the living room to the kitchen I got bowled over by the aroma of roast pork and fried apples. I followed it into the kitchen where my mother gave me the usual thorough once-over. Seeing no bloodstains or ruined clothes, she smiled. "Have a good time?"

I said "Swell" and told her, in case she hadn't noticed, that it was snowing and maybe getting cold enough to start freezing the ponds.

"High time!" she said. "You've been very patient with it."

My interest in the weather let me in for more witty remarks during dinner. My father said he wished I'd given him another month without having to put the chains on the car. Aunt Lizzie complained that with all the cold-weather clothes coming out of storage all over the school district her classroom was going to smell like mothballs for a week and it was all my fault.

Uncle Art said he was thinking of paying me a commission for driving a lot of men into the store to keep warm while they waited for the streetcar. "If I can't sell every one of them a cigar," he said, "or a package of gum, I ought to get out of the business."

I said ten percent should be about right.

"Ten percent!" He wagged his head sadly, looking at my mother. "That's a greedy, grasping boy you've let loose upon this world."

I looked across the table at Felice and said, "Haven't *you* got any funny remarks to make?"

"What?" She looked sort of startled. Hadn't heard any of this. Probably outlining a great work of art in her head.

I excused myself and went out to the kitchen with my dishes. Then I eased out through the back porch to see if it was still snowing. It was. The flakes were bigger than before and the wind had let up. Everything was white now and mysterious and still. It was exciting too, the kind of excitement that grabs you around the chest and squeezes. Sometimes it's like one of those dreams where you know something terrific's about to happen but you don't know what and think you'll die if you don't find out.

Only this wasn't a dream. The snow was real, the cold too. All the forces of nature were going my way—finally. I could feel every move I would make, skimming over the ice on my skates, effortlessly controlling the puck, one eye on the crouching goalie, who didn't have a prayer of blocking the shot that would be rocketing toward him, a blurred black streak over the ice.

I wallowed around in this daydream all the time I

was drying dishes while Felice washed them. She must have been locked up in her own world too. We hardly spoke at all; the only conversation I can remember went like this:

Felice, picking up glass bowl: "You call this dry?"

Me, peering with imaginary magnifying glass: "Look again in thirty seconds. Evaporation."

Felice: "Clever, clever, clever!"

Free at last, I wandered up to my room, taking my dream world with me.

Ed and I had got started hitching rides in small ways back when we were ten, badgering Uncle Art into letting us hitch onto his Model T for a couple of blocks at about three miles an hour. That got too tame in a hurry and meant we were just about forced to go out and find rides with people we didn't know, usually in front of stores and such places where there was always a lot of coming and going. By the time the second winter was over we'd learned a lot from experience, some of it painful, or scary, or both. Like getting dragged across manhole covers, which are always bare iron because it's warmer down below. Same with streetcar tracks or thawed patches of pavement. When you hit one, sparks fly from your sled runners and the sudden drag on your arm—the one holding onto the bumper—feels like your shoulder's being dislocated. If the drag lasts more than two or three seconds you'll either let go and take your chances on what's coming behind, or get yanked off your sled. We soon learned to avoid some of these hazards by edging out from behind the back wheel to keep an eye on what was coming.

By the next winter we were really experts, taking

longer rides, getting farther and farther from home. You can always get home, or near it, if you know your way around, which we sure got so we did.

Ed and I agreed there was nothing like it for thrills, speed, and , well, danger; to myself I don't deny that, and neither does he. And by this year I was more eager than ever to get started because this would be the last winter ever.

I was enjoying all that daydreaming so much that I used up a month's supply of strength of character to get out my algebra book and settle down to work on the test Miss Wolfinger had threatened us with. The only comforting thing about studying for Algebra was that if I got really stuck Aunt Lizzie was nearly always around to straighten me out.

CHAPTER

4

A Job with a Bonus

SCHOOL NEXT DAY was pure torture. Except for algebra class, that is—in spite of the test. In that class my desk was two rows over and one behind Judy Felton's, so that I could see her hair and one ear all the time, the side of her face some of the time—when she turned to whisper to Amy Jaeger—and all of her face once in a while when she turned around to squelch Jerry Burke, who thought he was a comedian and should have been squelched with a ball bat. When she turned like that I usually managed to be frowning over an equation, but a time or two she caught my eye and I felt myself turning the color of a boiled tomato. The second time it happened she smiled. I knew she had to be smiling at somebody behind me, but I did my tomato impersonation anyway.

The *rest* of the school day was torture anyhow because Ed and I had arranged to go sliding on the Center Street hill right after school, and while it couldn't hold a candle to hitching rides, I was still eager. To our disgust the snow had stopped sometime during the night so there were only eight or ten inches on the ground, not nearly enough to put a good solid layer on the streets once it got packed down by the traffic. The next best thing was to go to the Center Street hill.

It's the steepest hill anywhere near our neighborhood and when conditions are right the city ropes off the side streets from Thirty-ninth east to Thirty-sixth, so the kids can slide the whole way without worrying about cars.

After school I made fast tracks for home and changed my pants while eating a stale cinnamon roll which was all I could find in the kitchen. I wouldn't have taken the time to change if my mother hadn't made me take off my school pants and put on my old corduroys.

Because of all the delay, when I got out to the end of our drive Ed was already there. He was putting in the time by buffing his sled runners with a square of carborundum paper. We greeted each other by grumbling about the weather for lifting our hopes so high and then letting them drop. Then we headed south, carrying our sleds diagonally across our backs, the runners sticking out. As we passed the front of Weinstocks' I got my usual stab of guilt when I thought about Mr. Weinstock and I said, "That's what I *ought* to be doing—shoveling their walks."

"Shovel 'em later."

Ignoring that, I said, "It might give me a chance to—you know—*talk* to him."

Ed groaned. "You still in a sweat about *that*? You could've done it any time last month!"

"Easy for you to say—you don't have to do it."

He gave me a disgusted look and said, "You wouldn't have to do it either if you hadn't got that nutty idea in your head." He shook his head sort of pityingly and added, "End of the world!"

"You wouldn't be so high and mighty," I said, "if you weren't plain pig-ignorant! There's plenty of big brains behind this thing, guys with long strings of college degrees who've written a lot of books and lectured all over the place."

"Like Albert Einstein? Anybody asked him his opinion?"

"How should I know? But plenty of others, and I've learned enough to know that if I get straight with Mister Weinstock and . . . and the other things, I'm going to feel great when—all right, *if*—it happens."

"If it *happens*? Look, if it *happens* you won't feel anything at all. Not if the whole shebang goes boom and disappears!" He was getting as heated up as I was. "And anyway, I want to know how all these big brains can suddenly know for sure it's going to happen on a certain day—or any other time."

By then we'd got to Iola and crossed to the other side of Thirty-fifth where we put our sleds down and knelt on them, ready to start the gradual slide to Rollins Street, two blocks farther along. But we didn't shove off, just went on talking in a kneeling position. Or anyway, *I* did. "They didn't do anything *suddenly*." My turn to be scornful. "They'd been studying and calculating about it for years and years."

It was fool luck that I knew so much about it. A couple of days ago I'd come across an article in *Collier's* magazine about this minister back east who had originated the study. Because his name was so peculiar I remembered it—Lucius DeVore Mergen-breit—and it had a string of initials after it showing he was a doctor of divinity, master of a few other things, and dean of a big church in Philadelphia, as well as professor of theology at a big university. The article told about how he and his students, or disciples or whatever they were, had been studying what they called the "apocalyptic writings" for a long time before they made their announcement to the world. Then some other authorities joined them and backed up their opinions.

I remembered enough to explain to Ed that they'd started with the books of Daniel and Revelation and worked their way through a mountain of other writings in various ancient languages as well as more modern things. Then they'd boiled it all down and mixed in a batch of mathematical and astronomical calculations, plus a few hints from The Great Beyond, arrived at through prayer and meditation. The results, when they finally sent them out to the religious press and then the regular press, were "virtually unassailable," according to the article.

While Ed thought that over we started down the easy slope, and when we got to the bottom and started walking again he said, "Well, I got to admit those guys know a lot more than I do, but I guess unless I get to understanding it better I'll just go on enjoying my ignorance while it lasts."

I had a comment to make about that but before I could get the first word out he suddenly grabbed me by the arm, bringing us both to a halt. "Hey! It's snowing!"

Darned if it wasn't. We'd been so hot in the head

and churned up with our dumb argument we hadn't even noticed when it began, but now it was coming down at a good rate—big, swift flakes that could pile up in a hurry. I said, "Wow! Maybe this time we'll get enough to do us some good."

"Got my fingers crossed," Ed said as we put on a little speed, heading for the Center Street hill and kicking up little puffs of snow at each step, just for the fun of it.

At the corner we peered toward the hill. Thanks to the falling snow it was like looking through a curtain of cheesecloth, so we couldn't see the top of the hill at all, but halfway down figure after figure began to appear. There were dozens of kids in the street, some zipping down, others trudging up. It was plain to see the barricades were up at the side streets, closing the hill to car traffic. In about two minutes we joined the trudgers.

It's not the steepest hill you ever saw, but steep enough so that you're blowing clouds of frosty air by the time you get to the top. What's important is that it's steep enough to take you down with a sizzling speed that makes it worth the climb.

It was just zip down, plod up, stand around a while catching our breath, then off again. Going up, we talked about a little bit of everything. Ed and I always have plenty to talk about, even if we can't remember half of it an hour later. This time all I could remember was that we'd steered clear of any more talk about the end of the world.

No telling how many trips we made, or how long it all took, but eventually we started noticing there were fewer and fewer kids on the hill and it was getting harder to see the ones that remained. Finally the steetlights came on and we took one more slide and headed for home.

The snow had slacked off a little by the time we reached the Rollins Street corner where business looked pretty brisk at the Piggly Wiggly and the drugstore. Cars were parked near all four corners of the intersection, heading in every direction. We came to a quick stop, as if we'd dropped our anchors. Ed looked at me. I looked back. He said, "Just a quick one? See how it goes?" I took another look around. On the sidewalk the new snow was five or six inches deep, loose and fluffy, but on the street it looked as if there'd been enough traffic to pack it down pretty well on top of last night's.

"Well, why not?" I said. Putty in the hands of temptation. How could I know it was the worst decision I'd ever made in my life?

Pointing to a Cadillac sedan facing south, Ed said, "Down to Ingersoll and back?" I nodded and we eased over to the telephone pole a few feet from the Cadillac and leaned against it after laying our sleds down flat. Just a couple of kids with nothing to do but shoot the breeze.

In about two minutes a man with a grocery sack came hurrying out, heading straight for the Cadillac. By the time he'd got in and slammed the door he had two freeloaders hanging onto his rear bumper, one on each side. The engine rumbled into life, and here came the old sweet-sick odor of partly burned gas, then the tug on the arm we knew so well, the crunch of chained tires, and we were moving. Slowly, then faster, then faster. This was what we'd been dreaming of for all these months.

We had about one whole minute to enjoy it before the world turned inside out.

At first everything was about normal except that the car's motion seemed to be blowing more loose snow in my face than usual. As we gradually picked up speed there was more. Pretty soon I took a quick backwards look as I always did, to see what was coming back there. But—shock number one—I couldn't *tell*. There were lights, but they were blurred by whirling snow, like lights seen through fog, and they could have come from anywhere—car headlights, streetlights, what-ever.

Then I eased my sled to the left, to sight along the side of the car and see what was ahead. What I saw was another light, blurry as the ones behind but growing, getting brighter. Oncoming car!

It went past with a *whoosh* and a flash of purer light and then—shock number two—for a few seconds I was alone in a dark hole. I could see my mitten and the section of bumper it grasped, but I couldn't see Ed, who was only four or five feet away. Unless he'd panicked and let go.

For those few endless moments I was a blind man speeding full tilt through streets where he'd never been. It was like the kind of nightmare where you wake up screaming.

Then the darkness gave way grudgingly. Another glance showed me Ed was still there, his whole body looking rigid as an ax handle. He didn't look my way.

Fear did it, I suppose, but for once my mind was

suddenly clearer than the world around me and I knew what was happening. All moving cars were sucking up the loose new-fallen snow from the thin compacted layer beneath, each carrying its own blizzard along, white whirlwinds that thickened the air and smothered light.

Fat lot of good it did to figure all that out. The fact was that, on a sudden impulse and without stopping to think, we'd got ourselves into the godawfulest jam we'd ever been in. We couldn't let go because we couldn't tell what was coming up behind. And we couldn't stay on because we'd have to survive another of those awful blackouts every time we met another car, and I didn't see how I could live through it. Forget about May Day; the end of my world, and Ed's, was waiting just up this street.

One of Uncle Art's favorite sayings came rocketing into my head: "Nothing is ever so bad it can't get worse."

Right away it did. I took another peek around the side and saw another fast-growing splash of light, but this one had a red look to it and was flashing. Warning light? Police? Trouble ahead?

In about one second the answer came. Part of it anyway. Through the bumper and into my arm came a surge of pressure. The driver had hit the brakes. He could see whatever was ahead, but I couldn't. It could be a block away or a hundred feet. *Now* we couldn't let go because our own momentum would drive us right under the car.

Then came a sickening swerve. Chains or no chains, the car was fighting the brakes, trying to skid. Instantly the pressure on my arm eased. Resumed, eased again. Good driver up there; he was pumping the brake pedal, fighting to stay in control while slowing. Comforting, but not when any moment could bring a thunderous crash to mash us into unimaginable shapes.

It didn't happen. The driver stayed in command, slowed the big car to a crawl, and eased to a stop at the curb. My first impulse was to shut my eyes and enjoy the absence of deathly fear. Then came the instinct of self-preservation which told me to get out of there as far and fast as possible. I couldn't see what had happened but there were voices ahead, hard policeman-like voices. The red light was pulsing, lighting the falling snow and the scene around. It lighted us too, and I assumed I must look just as ghastly as Ed did.

We didn't say a word, just picked up our sleds with arms that didn't feel up to the job and tried to look like shadows as we scrambled to the sidewalk and began the long walk home.

By the time we'd plowed our way back to Rollins where it all began we'd learned how to talk again and agreed on everything essential, such as that it was a miracle we weren't in a funeral parlor right now, and that we hoped somebody would shoot us if we ever even *thought* of going hitching again unless conditions were exactly right.

We also agreed we were starving and would probably have to go on starving until breakfast because we'd missed dinner by about an hour. It was hard to believe when we peered in the drugstore window that it was only twenty past five. I'd have sworn that whole awful ordeal had taken at least an hour, plus twenty minutes to walk back almost from Ingersoll, which was as far as we'd got. The rest of the way home we spent thinking up interesting reasons why we were as late as we were.

In front of my house we said "So long, see you tomorrow" just as if nothing out of the ordinary had happened. At the side door I toed my galoshes off and banged them against the side of the house the way I was supposed to, and set them on the stair landing inside before shedding my jacket and mittens and stuff. Right away I smelled tobacco smoke. Either my father or my uncle had been down in the furnace room smoking a cigar. They do it down there because my mother won't stand for it in the house. She says it makes her feel like she's living in a saloon, which is funny because she's never been inside a saloon.

The big room used to be called the laundry room, and my mother still does the washing back in the corner where there's a drain in the floor. Everyone forgets to call it the game room, which it became after my folks had replaced the old coal furnace with a fancy oil-burning one. At that time they'd cleaned the room all up, painted it in bright colors, and brought some old furniture down, including a sofa and the Victrola and a supply of records. There was also a dartboard on one wall and one of those miniature pool tables. It was a great place, especially in summer when the rest of the house is sweltering.

Anyway, on this occasion the cigar smell was noticeable in the game room but not really bad. My father's cigars are the worst, because they're five-cent Idolitas, while Uncle Art splurges on ten-centers and once in a while on a two-bit stogie when he's feeling flush.

I went on up to the kitchen, where it's a different world. This time the air was full of the smell of roasting meat. It couldn't smell better than that in heaven. My mother was real busy but she always takes time to give me a pretty good looking over. She said, "I don't know how you do it! You'd think there was a big sign up on the roof that lights up and says DINNER." Then she peered at me a little more closely and added, "Everything all right? You look a little . . ."

While she looked for the word she wanted I jumped right in. "A little messed up? No wonder; Ed and I and some other guys've been dumping each other's sleds up on the hill."

She gave a big sigh and said, "If I can just raise you till you're old enough to vote I won't ask for more. Go get your hands washed." She was forgetting about the end of the world, and I didn't mention it.

While we ate, my father and Uncle Art were talking about the sorry state of things somewhere—Washington, probably. My mother and Felice were talking about redecorating her room. I was concentrating on making sure I ate my share of everything, and in the middle of it all the phone rang.

Felice was up and into the breakfast room like a shot, leaving the swinging door to flop itself shut behind her. She always hopes the phone will be for her—one of her gabby friends—and if it is you probably won't see her again for half an hour. But this time she shoved the door open a little and said, sounding disappointed, "Timmie, it's for you."

I thought it would be Ed, but it wasn't; it was a guy named Carl Simons who was eighth-grade president and on the debating team among other things. He said, "Tim, I just got handed the job of putting out the spring issue of the *Highlight*. Literary edition, you know. I'm getting a bunch together to do it. Miss Wilson said you were one of the best English students, and I'd sure like to have you help out."

This wasn't my idea of good news. It sounded like a lot of trouble I didn't need. I said, "Gee, I don't know. I may be good at English but I'm lousy at math and I've got about all I can handle just trying to keep up."

Maybe this sounded as feeble to him as it did to me. Anyway, he wasn't going to give up easy. He said, "Well, it's not like you'd have to do it all yourself. I've already lined up some good people: Liza Greene . . . Joe Franklin . . . Judy Felton . . ."

I think he mentioned some other names but I'd stopped listening. I said, "Oh," which meant a lot more than it sounds like, and he went on, "I'd like to get going right away. Deadline's April fifteenth. I sure hope you can help us out. I thought I'd hold a meeting at my house during Christmas vacation and start the ball rolling."

He didn't need to try so hard. He already had me hooked, netted, and into the boat. I said, "I don't know how much help I'll be, but I'll give it a try."

He said, "Great! Can you make it next Thursday? Four o'clock?" He gave me his address and I wrote it down. He added, "My mother says she'll furnish cider and cookies."

"Fine," I said. "I'll be there." I'd have said the same if she was going to furnish pig's feet and parsnips.

When I went back to the dining room Uncle Art said, "Got yourself suckered into a job, did you?"

I said, "Boy! A person sure doesn't get any privacy around here!"

"You're telling *me!*" Felice said.

"The family," Aunt Lizzie chimed in, "is a public institution, not a private one."

"Bunch of malcontents." That was my father's contribution.

In the middle of all this I noticed everybody was still looking at me and finally my mother said, "Well, son, aren't you going to tell your non-private family what it was you got talked into?"

"Oh, nothing," I said. "This guy just asked me to help put out the spring issue of the school paper. It's sort of a literary issue."

Uncle Art said, "Ah. Recognition! Merit will out! Time will come when we can all brag we're related to the editor of the *Literary Digest.*"

"Arthur, stop teasing him!" my mother said. "It *is* recognition, and I'm sure he deserves it."

I said, "Oh, they just couldn't think of anyone else." Modesty, that was my strong suit, and I had plenty to be modest about, knowing I'd have weaseled out of the thing someway if Carl Simons hadn't spoken the magic name.

It wasn't until after dishwashing was over that I got the chance to go up to my room and panic in private. I felt like a guy who changes his mind after he's already jumped out of a tenth-story window. How was I going to get friendly with the prettiest girl I knew when I couldn't even *look* at her without melting down into my socks? And *kiss* her? They had padded cells for people like me, and the sooner they locked me into one the better.

CHAPTER

5

Coals of Fire

IF THINGS LIKE Christmas and weather variations hadn't got in the way I might have devoted the next week to thinking nonstop about Carl Simons's meeting and the unbelievable progress I'd be making with Judy Felton—or about Carl Simons's meeting and the incredibly dumb things I'd say to her and ruin everything.

Christmas was a pretty good distraction, though. I got my skates. Black shoes with brown steel-reinforced toes, blades welded to tubular steel frames in red baked enamel. I had sense enough not to act surprised, but I turned loose the enthusiastic thanks, and meant it. With a straight face my father said, "Well, that's a relief. We couldn't think *what* to give you, and decided on skates at the last minute. It was a gamble. Isn't that right, Nell!"

My mother said "Absolutely!" and everybody laughed except Grampa, who had been out on the road when my Santa letter arrived.

Felice's contribution was a pair of heavy wool socks

to go with the skates. "Maybe you'll need two pairs," my father said, "to fill them up. We got 'em with room to grow in. Just don't plan on growing feet the size of your uncle's."

"Not a chance," Uncle Art said, stretching his legs out and admiring his feet, which were wearing the deerskin house slippers Aunt Lizzie had given him. "Only one set of beauties like this allowed per family. Law of nature."

I wanted to put my skates on and at least walk around enough to see how they felt, but my mother put the kibosh on that idea in a hurry. "You're out of your mind, Timmie. On the *carpet?*"

I could see her point. Those blades were sharp enough to give you the shivers when you ran your thumb along the edges. So after all the presents had been opened and the excitement died down I put on outdoor clothes, including the new socks, and carried the skates out to the back porch, which is wooden, and put them on. Then I clumped down the steps, holding on to the railing. That was when the weather pulled the first of its surprises. Sometime while nobody was looking beyond the Christmas tree, it had started snowing and was coming down now at a pretty steady pace. The old snow was still on the ground but was covered already with the new, concealing the dog tracks and the sifting of black that came from the chimneys of neighbors who hadn't switched yet from coal to oil or gas.

I proceeded to mess up the backyard with tracks of my own as I stumbled around getting the feel of the skates. Then I made some more as I staggered over to the garage to look at the thermometer. I had to stretch myself out of shape to read the temperature without standing on the cement walk. Anything to keep from dulling those blades.

The mercury stood at twenty degrees. Not bad, but nowhere near low enough to freeze a four-inch layer of ice on a pond. I told myself to look again later to see if there was any chance, then went in and took off the skates, carefully wiping them, blades and all, and returning them to the box, with the top off. I put the box under the tree with the other stuff. If I couldn't use them I could at least look at them once in a while.

Pretty soon I got orders to go bring more firewood from the stack in the narrow place between our garage and the Swansons'. I made three trips and on the last one took another look at the thermometer. It said twenty-two degrees. Wrong direction! Anyway, it was still snowing.

By this time the house was full of roast turkey aroma; my mother, Felice, and Aunt Lizzie were clattering around in the kitchen and dining room and yelping at me to get out of the way; and I was suddenly starving.

Later, when the turkey looked like it had been in a war and Uncle Art had carried the remains out to the kitchen and everybody was eating mince pie and saying how stuffed they were, I happened to look toward the windows behind my mother's chair. I did a sort of doubletake, like Oliver Hardy, and said, "Hey look—the snow's stopped!"

It had for sure, and the ground and all the rooftops were dazzling white under the sun that had come out. My father said, "Clearing in the east. Means colder tonight—or maybe warmer. Sure sign."

He leaned back, patting his belly as if it were the size of Santa Claus's. "Art, what say we let this great dinner settle a bit, then get out the snow shovels? Be finished before dark."

Uncle Art groaned. "Maybe I'll get me a room at the Y. Pray a little, get fed, no chores."

"They have cooks like this down at the Y?" my father asked.

"Hmmm," said Uncle Art. "I take your point."

A few seconds passed and I said, "*I'll* help shovel!" I'll take shoveling over doing dishes any time.

I couldn't have got more attention by spitting on the floor. Everybody was staring at me, which was no surprise because it's well known that the only walks I ever shoveled belonged to other people. Cash on the barrelhead. My mother, naturally, was the first to get over the shock. "Nice try, Timmie," she said, "but there's a lovely clean dishtowel waiting for you in the kitchen."

I don't know why I tried it. Nothing like that had ever worked yet. I said, "Well, maybe this once Uncle Art could—"

Tossing his napkin onto the table, Uncle Art interrupted, "Oh no you don't!" Then, to the room in general, "Crafty little urchin wants to stick me with KP!" He lunged to his feet. "Come on, Frank, let's get shoveling!"

Telling myself anything was worth trying once, I loaded myself with dirty dishes and headed for the kitchen.

While Felice and I slaved away I turned my mind off to everything but the meeting on Thursday. I pictured myself sitting across from Judy at a small table—better yet, *next* to her, on a sofa maybe, while I outlined a few of the great ideas I had for the literary edition. Her eyes were glued to my face, those lips . . .

"What in the world's the matter with you?" Felice didn't sound anything like Judy Felton.

"Whadda you mean what's the matter with me? *Nothing's* the matter with me!"

"Then why are you drying that plate for the *third time*?"

"I wasn't."

"I *saw* you!"

I mumbled something about having a lot on my mind and decided I'd better do my daydreaming while I was alone. This was Saturday. Five days to go before the meeting, which was time enough to dream myself into real trouble. And after *that* I could start dreaming up a broken jaw for myself. First boxing lesson.

The weather cooperated in spreading my attention around a little. That night it snowed some more. Not enough, but heading in the right direction. I checked the weather story the next day in the *Sunday Register and Tribune*. It said things like "possible light snowfall Monday" and "Low tonight 16–18 degrees." It was beginning to look like a race between ice skating and snow for hitching.

Since I couldn't hurry either one I went to find some walks to shovel—make a little money. Ordinarily I'd have started with Weinstocks'. I *wanted* to start with Weinstocks'—I wanted like anything to say what I had to say to him, get the whole thing off my mind and crossed off Miss Wilson's list. Well, I didn't. I started across the street with the Greiders', telling myself I'd end up with Weinstocks', absolutely, and no more weaseling out. To punish myself for losing my nerve this last time, I shoveled Greiders' at about twice my usual speed, then went on to the big house on the corner, then the next house west on Iola. And all the time I kept seeing Mr. Weinstock's face that morning way back in early December instead of the snow in front of me.

The Weinstocks live next door to us and they're my oldest snow-shoveling customers. First time I did their walks I was about ten, I guess—anyhow, too puny to handle a big shovel full of wet snow. I probably did a lousy job. Mr. Weinstock paid me two bits anyway, same as if it'd been just fine, and told me it looked dandy. It made me feel grown-up. Valuable. I never had felt that valuable before. I didn't know until a lot later that he'd called my mother and asked her if it was okay to let "such a little boy work so hard." Another thing I didn't know was that my father had gone over to their house after I was in bed and fixed the walks right. I don't need any help now. I must've scooped tons of snow off miles of walks by this time.

Well, anyhow, I've shoveled the Weinstocks' sidewalks ever since. I like to. I mean, they're *friends* of mine. More than that, really, because I get the feeling they sort of think I belong to them. My mother says it's partly because they don't have any kids of their own and never will have. It all adds up to plenty of reason for me to feel so rotten about what I did.

It was an ordinary school morning except that the front tire on my bike had gone flat and I had to walk. If I'd been riding none of it would have happened. I'd no sooner got outdoors than I saw Mr. Weinstock out in front of his house, bending over and looking down at the sidewalk. That was strange enough in itself because ordinarily they both would have left for work by that time. He's a partner in a downtown jewelry store and Mrs. Weinstock works at the Jewish Community Center, which is on the north side of town. I think she's boss of the place.

He was dressed for business as usual and had his back toward me. I'd gone only a few steps in his direction when he moved a little and I could see there was a bucket in front of him which he was dipping into with a push-broom and scrubbing away at the cement. He couldn't see me of course, and I had rubber soles, so he couldn't hear me either.

Naturally I was about as curious as I could get, but there wasn't a clue to what he was up to. I'd got to within maybe ten feet when my nose caught the first clue. Turpentine. The clue was no help.

Now I was so close I had to let him know I was there so as not to scare him. I made a little throat-clearing noise. It scared him anyway. He straightened up like he'd had an electric shock, and I said, "Good morning, Mr. Weinstock." It came out in a kind of squeak. It sounded funny to me, so it should have sounded the same to him, but when he jerked around he looked anything but amused. Instead he looked sort of stricken, as if he'd seen the ghost of his grandfather or something. Scared too, maybe. And ashamed.

There was no way I could keep my eyes away from what was there on the sidewalk. Big black letters made with paint. The turpentine scrubbing had done nothing but fuzz the letters around the edges. They were easy to read and they said DIRTY KIKE. The shock of reading it felt like a kick in the stomach, so what must it have felt like to him? All I could do at the moment was wish I was whizzing past on my bike, wish I didn't know how to read, wish I didn't know what that ugly word meant, wish I was sick in bed, wish I could do anything in the world but stand there and look into those sad, dark eyes in a face that was trying to smile. He even did smile, a little bit, and he said, like he was apologizing, "The kids, they play tricks."

I felt sure he didn't believe it was kids, and neither did I. It was grown-up white men who hated black men and Jews and anybody else who didn't think or look just like themselves. I'd seen pictures in the paper of the Ku Klux Klan burning huge crosses on the Statehouse lawn when the government had done something they didn't like. I understood the kind of wickedness that had painted those words. And what did I do—me, Timothy Andrew Walden who never in his life would be called a name like that—what did I do?

Without quite looking straight at him I gave him a dumb, sick smile, like I was too weak in the head to know a real nastiness when I saw it, like it didn't have anything to do with me, and made a big show of shifting my schoolbooks from one arm to the other. Then, carefully avoiding another glance at the side-walk, I mumbled a lot of garbage about having to hurry or I'd be late for school, and seeing him later. And I turned my back and hightailed it down the street like the hound of the Baskervilles was after me.

But no hound could have ripped me up more savagely than my conscience was doing by the time I'd scuttled down to Crocker Street and turned the corner.

I was putting up a defense, but it was so feeble I needn't have bothered. I asked my conscience what I could have *done*; I just didn't know how to handle a situation like that. I was just a kid and Mr. Weinstock was a grown man, so it was up to him. And I did have to get to school, didn't I? This got me another jab of the pitchfork and my conscience said, "You're going to get horsewhipped or something if you're five minutes late—or an hour as far as that goes? You could have stayed and helped. You weren't wearing a business suit. You could have got down on your knees and scrubbed like fury. You could have at least messed it up enough so nobody could read it, and you'd feel on top of the world now instead of like something the dog threw up."

It didn't stop there either. It reminded me of all the times I'd mowed the Weinstocks' lawn last summer and how he'd always added a dime to the agreed-on price. And how on hot days while I worked Mrs. Weinstock would come out with a bottle of pop and make me sit in the shade while I drank it.

After that it got rough, my conscience. It called me a yellow dog and then apologized to the dog because *it* wouldn't have known what it was doing. It said I was no better than the scum who passed by the hurt man who later was saved by the Good Samaritan. It said I ought to go hide my head so people wouldn't get sick from looking at me. My conscience always has had a way with words.

To round things off it told me that pretending I didn't understand the meaning of the message on the sidewalk was just the same as *agreeing* with it. It said that until I did something—*soon*—to get myself straight with Mr. Weinstock, man to man, it would be not only obliged but *happy* to make the rest of my life a misery.

And here it was nearly three weeks closer to the end of the world and I still hadn't done a thing.

By the time I'd shoveled what felt like four miles of sidewalks I'd made a decision. This was the day I'd apologize. What was I so scared of anyway?

The minute I arrived at the Weinstocks' property line I started in shoveling, hardly noticing I was pooped already. It seemed no time at all until I was finished, standing on the front stoop and knocking on the glass of the storm door. I was also hoping like mad that Mrs. Weinstock would open the door instead of him.

No such luck. The inside door gave its usual little shudder and groan as it opened, and there was Sam Weinstock, with his little black pipe stuck into the middle of his smile. He's a small, neat man with black hair that tends to curl and make him look younger than he is. He was wearing his blue velvet smoking jacket with black lapels and a kind of sash, which would have looked show-offish on most men but not on him.

He already had his scuffed-up little leather purse in his hand when he pushed open the storm door. "Come in, Timmie, come in! You had a nice Christmas, yes?" Without waiting for an answer he looked past me to the front walk. "Nice job, Timmie, always a nice job." He began poking around in the purse and peering into it.

I gulped air. Now was the time. *Say it,* I told myself. *Go on!*

What I said was, "The, uh, paper said it might snow a little tomorrow. I'll come sweep it off, if it does. No charge."

"Giving away labor?" he said, pretending to be real surprised. "Rich you won't get!" Then he lighted up again with the smile. "But I accept—I accept!" He dug into the purse with two fingers and gave me the quarter he owed me and added another dime, the way he always did. "You're a good boy, Timmie. It's a pleasure to do business with you."

I mumbled a feeble thank-you and started home feeling more like a dirty dishrag than ever. My great burst of resolution had lasted about twenty seconds. *Why,* I asked myself, did he have to go on being so doggone *nice* to me?

Things not being lousy enough, I planted a big overshoe smack in the middle of those words painted there on the sidewalk. They hadn't changed from the last time I'd looked—smudged around the edges and faint, but I knew what they said. I thought—and not for the first time—that if I couldn't *talk* to Mr. Weinstock about how I felt there must be something I could *do*, something that would make amends without words. But what? No answer.

I was so disgusted with myself that I'd got clear into our garage, hanging the shovel on its hook, before I remembered to count my hard-earned money. This alone proved I wasn't in my normal state of mind, so

I emptied my pockets and totaled up. One dollar and twenty cents. Five minutes later when my mother asked me how much money I'd made I did my absentminded act. "Oh, about fifty cents."

This was a matter of self-defense because she doesn't believe my money is for spending. It's for putting into the savings bank where it will earn interest, and the interest will earn more interest, so that if I never take any of it out, by the time I'm about ninety-seven I'll be rich.

The result was a sort of secret civil war between my mother and me. Who's winning I'm not sure, but I manage to hang on to enough money—just barely—to buy the necessities of life. On the other hand I'm always surprised when I make a deposit at how much the interest keeps adding up in my bank book.

Suddenly, I thought about what would happen to all that money, and it was like a slosh of ice water in the face. Whatever was in my bank account on May Day would be there forever. I don't know why, until then, I'd never once thought about that.

Or the bank itself might disappear—all the banks in the world—and there wouldn't be such a thing as money. Right then another idea hit me with a shock that was more like electricity than ice water. The answer! Go down to the bank while it was still there and take all my money out. And *spend* it.

I'd hardly got started on that useful line of thinking when dinner was called, which took my mind off money, but later I got back to it. How big a bulge would sixty-five one-dollar bills make in my pocket? A thing like that can really push my button and I dizzied around in a fever of spending, progressing in a hurry from ordinary run-of-the-mill buying of hamburgers and chocolate milkshakes, with Juicy Fruit chewing gum afterwards, to real deluxe daydreams. The main feature in these was me taking Judy Felton to lunch at some swanky place like the Des Moines Club, which I'd heard of but never set foot in, and after that to whatever movie theater she wanted to go to. With a whole afternoon we might even get around to *two* theaters. After all that I could hardly stoop to taking her home in a smelly old streetcar, so we'd go in a taxi. It might cost as much as fifty cents, but it would be worth it.

Me taking Judy Felton anywhere in a taxi was crazy, but no crazier then going to the bank and stuffing my pockets with the money that would never have been there in the first place if it weren't for my mother. In a way it was as much her money as mine—more so, even. So if it stayed right where it was and evaporated on May Day, at least I wouldn't have spent the meantime feeling like a thief.

Having got a grip on myself, I opened my notebook to make a list of all the brilliant literary ideas that were going to bring me forcefully to Judy's attention at the coming meeting.

Half an hour or so later the sheet of paper was as clean as it had ever been. But as things turned out it didn't matter because—little did I know—my lucky stars, or Fate, or whatever, were already putting together a series of coincidences that would do the job without my having to be any more brilliant than the cheese in a rattrap.

CHAPTER

6

Genius at Work

SLEEP WAS SLINKING up behind me that night, sort of whispering and offering me a fuzzy little picture to look at. It showed my overshoe smack in the middle of those smeary words on the Weinstocks' sidewalk, and I was telling myself it looked real pretty but what did it have to do with me. And then Fate said (I heard it distinctly), "What if that wasn't an overshoe? What if it was a baseball shoe, or a golf shoe—something *abrasive*?"

There it was—slam! bang! Eureka! I was out of bed like a shot and grabbing for my pants. In about a minute and a half I was sneaking down the hall, quiet as a burglar, toward Felice's door. Waking her up to ask a big favor didn't strike me as the brightest way to go at a project like this, but she was my only hope.

Scrabbling on the door with my fingernails I said in a near whisper, "It's me. Can I talk to you?"

There was a rustle, a shuffle, then her voice, sounding resigned. "It better be important."

"It is—*vitally*." The door opened and I was relieved

to see she hadn't even got ready for bed. She shut the door behind me and plunked herself down on her desk chair. "So all right. Talk!"

"I got to do something—right now—and I need help, and there's no one but you who can do it."

"What are you whispering for?"

I was only half-whispering, but this was no time to argue. "Because if they hear us they'll get nosy and end up thinking of a million reasons why we shouldn't do it."

"Bet I'll think of a few myself." I noticed she'd lowered her voice, and that was a good sign. "Well, go on—what's the big deal?"

Talking about as fast as the auctioneer at the stock-yards, I sketched the story of how I'd disgraced myself with Mr. Weinstock and suffered about it and fallen on my face every time I tried to do something about it until now—about five minutes ago—I'd had a brain-storm about what to do, and . . .

I might as well have not started on the second half of it because I'd no more than said what was painted there on the sidewalk than Felice stiffened and got this horrified look on her face. She burst out, "Is *that* what that smudgy place is? Well, what kind of a slimy, scummy chunk of"—I stuck a warning finger to my lips and she quieted down a little—"chunk of garbage would do a thing like that to that *sweet* little man! If I ever find out I'll report him to the police because there must be a law against something like that." She took a new supply of air. "Defacing public property, that's what it is—and that's a crime! And another thing—about calling people names in public. It's—it's *slander,* and they can get sued for it!"

Well, I'd known she'd be indignant, but all this fire-eating took me by surprise and I tried to cool her down by saying I didn't think Mr. Weinstock would want to sue anybody, or get the police into it either. Felice jumped up and said, "Well, just tell me what I'm supposed to do and—and I'll *do* it."

First I told her what I had to do myself, then her part of it. I watched while the wheels went around in her head and ended in a smile that said maybe my idea wasn't nutty at all. "Okay," she said. "You go get started. I'll get together the things I'll need."

"Give me half an hour," I said. "And wear plenty of warm stuff—there's an iceberg factory out there." She didn't even see me ease the door open and shut it silently behind me because she'd opened the lid of the big wooden chest where she keeps a lot of her art supplies and was doing a fast survey of its contents.

I made it all the way down to the basement stair landing without setting off a hue and cry and put on all the clothes I could find, including an old pair of pants my father wore for working around the place. With the flashlight from a hook in the doorframe, I was ready for anything this side of the Arctic Circle.

First use for the flashlight was to find the wire brush my father kept on a shelf in the garage and used to take the rust off metal things and old paint off wood.

Before you could say subzero I was down on my knees in front of the Weinstocks' house scrubbing away at those smudged-up black words. Until I got used to it, the sound I made—a scratchy *whisha-whisha-whisha*—sounded louder than it really was, but not loud enough to be heard inside a house. Whatever other sounds there were came from far off—the screech of a trolley as the streetcar made a tight turn, the chugging of a switch engine shunting freight cars around in the yards way over on the east side, the occasional clatter of tire chains blocks away. In my own little corner of the city, nothing moved but me or made any sound at all. It was sort of eerie, particularly under the strange glow of what I always think of as snowlight. There are two kinds—one when the moon and stars are out, throwing pale light down onto the snow-covered ground; the other, like this time, when a low layer of clouds catches all the lights of the city and reflects them down onto the snow to make a faint imitation of daylight.

Because it's an eerie sort of light I had to start imagining eerie things. Like what it was going to be like when there wasn't any light from the city. Maybe not as dark as a coal mine or a tomb, but too dark for a person to find his way around, and anyway, no person there to try. I wished my imagination wouldn't give me such a lonely time.

But right now there *was* snowlight, and it let me know after about five minutes of hard scrubbing that I was making progress. The area I'd worked over had already turned from smudgy black to dirty gray which grew even lighter when I put my mouth down close and blew away the grit those steel bristles were ripping loose from the concrete surface. I took a deep breath of glacial air and started in again.

A few breaths farther along I realized that instead of freezing I was starting to sweat a little, except for my feet and nose, which weren't doing any of the work. I kept at it. No chance to do anything else now anyway. I lost track of time. Had I been at this for an hour? Two hours? Nothing like that of course, as I realized when I jumped at the sound of footsteps behind me. Felice's voice asked, "You planning to gouge a hole all the way *through* that thing?"

Switching on the light I took a quick look. No hole, of course, but the big black smudge was gone, leaving a rectangle about two feet by ten inches that seemed almost dead white against the old concrete around it. There was grit all around and I was brushing away at it with the back of a mitten when Felice dropped down beside me, nudging me to one side as she did it. From somewhere she produced, magician-style, a little whiskbroom.

"Figured you wouldn't think of this." Since I hadn't, there was nothing I could say so I kept quiet while the artist nudged me a little farther out of her way and got to work with her little broom.

Now she opened the rectangular box she'd brought along and slid out a blue extra-thick stick of chalk. She began drawing in short fast strokes a horizontal line across the top of my clean rectangle. I asked could I hold the flashlight for her and she said, "Maybe later," and went on drawing blue lines as straight as if they'd been ruled until she'd outlined the whole rectangle. Then she put the blue chalk to one side, slid out a red one and said, "Now! What I really wish you'd do is build me a nice little bonfire because what I've got to do next is *take off this glove,* and if my hand freezes and they have to amputate it I'll never forgive you as long as I live!"

"Tell you what!" I said. Another inspiration. "I'll keep my hand stuck into my armpit till you say 'mitten,' then I'll yank my mitten off and you stick your hand in it and warm up a little. Then draw some more while I warm up the mitten again."

And that's the way we did it. Every time she said "Mitten!" we'd make the exchange at frantic speed. If anybody'd been watching it would have looked like some silly kind of game invented for nitwits, so of course we got silly and started counting the movements out like soldiers marching. "HUP-hoo-hree-foh!" Crazy, but I found myself thinking maybe for the first time ever that I was really lucky to have her for a sister.

Between the silly spells she worked like a demon with her chalks, while I watched, line by line, letter by letter, color by color, as she turned the three words which had been my only suggestion into something to admire and marvel at. In the end she said, "There!" slipped her own glove back on, put the chalks back into the box, and stood up. I kept looking down and saying, "Gee, Felice! Gee! It's beautiful!"

And it was. Inside the blue outline was a white one, then a red. In the middle were three words, printed in big block letters in mixed colors—blue, white, and red. Between the two rows of letters was a row of stars, and *they* were red, white, and blue, same as the letters. It looked like this:

SAM WEINSTOCK

*** *** ***

AMERICAN

After a few seconds Felice tucked her box under an arm and said briskly, "Well, you can stand here all night and freeze to death if you want to; *I'm* going home and thaw out!" Before she could carry this out I felt a tickling on my nose and cheeks and looked quickly toward the streetlight at the corner of Iola. The air was alive with a swirl of tiny dots. Snow!

"Uh oh!" Felice blurted. "By morning our work of art will be buried. How's Mr. Weinstock going to know it's there?"

"I'll get one of those old suitboxes out of the basement and cover it up. Then I'll be out here at the crack of dawn to uncover it. I was going to sweep the walks anyway." Tim Waldon, lightning thinker.

It didn't work out quite that way, but near enough. The main difference was that I hadn't planned to wake up a lot earlier than I needed to. What woke me was a sound I hadn't heard for a year and which for a few half-awake moments I couldn't identify. Coming from way down the street, it was at the same time a screech and a scrunch—eerie and endless.

In a couple of seconds a handful of facts assembled themselves. It was the milk wagon laboring up the slope from Crocker to Iola—a block and a half away yet, but the shriek of those iron tires on the packed snow was enough to wake a corpse. I couldn't hear the tread of the big white horse because the new snow cushioned it while the wheels crunched right through the new snow and mashed into the already-packed old snow, setting off the screech I was hearing. That sound told me the temperature had dropped a lot since Felice and I had sneaked back into the house and gone to bed. You can almost guess the temperature by the sound—the screechier the colder. As it came nearer I could hear the metallic jingle of bottles in the wire basket the milkman carries. The jingle of the full bottles accompanied the crunch of his boots as he hurried up a snow-covered driveway, and the empties rattled on a different note as he trotted back.

I'd often thought it would be nice to be a milkman or his horse on summer mornings with the birds singing away and the sun just up but not yet hot, and no cars or people to bother you. But on this kind of pitch-dark morning it would be a terrible job. Just thinking about it made me cold and I pulled up the extra blanket I hadn't needed when I went to bed.

While the sounds of the milk wagon faded and finally dwindled into silence I lay there getting warmer under the extra blanket and thinking I should go down and bring the milk in. If I didn't, my mother would find the bottles with columns of frozen cream sticking up about four inches beyond the bottle necks with the little pasteboard caps sitting on top like flat hats. The milk would thaw out all right but be sort of grainy and not taste right.

While I was thinking about doing this I went to sleep. Next thing I knew I was being shaken by the shoulder and Felice was saying "Wake up! Wake up! Wake up!" a lot more times than there was any need to. This was the only night ever that I'd waked up more times than I'd gone to sleep.

I lunged to a sitting position. "What's up?"

"It's almost *seven o'clock*! It snowed about two inches, so if you're going to sweep off the walk at Weinstocks' and uncover our artwork you'd better get at it!"

I couldn't have got dressed and out of there in less time if the house had been burning down. On the basement landing I'd no more than got started putting on all the outdoor clothes I could find than my father and Uncle Art came whuffing and stomping in, encased in leaky bubbles of arctic air and giving off powerful fumes of denatured alcohol. This told me they'd been out warming up the engine of the Essex, running it until the radiator warmed up enough to start boiling over because, as Uncle Art always put it, it was "under the influence of alcohol."

They both looked at me like I was the two-headed Tasmanian from the freak show and my father said, "Great glory, boy—you're not going out shoveling walks on a morning like this? It's fifteen below zero!"

"Not shoveling," I said, "just sweeping. For Mr. Weinstock. I promised him. It won't take long."

"Won't take long to freeze either," Uncle Art said. "If you make it home you'll need an icepick to undo your buttons."

"Can't help it," I said, sitting on a step to pull on my galoshes. "It was a promise."

"A promise!" echoed Uncle Art. "Holy everything, Frank—you suppose this family's nourishing a saint in its bosom?"

A second after they'd clattered up to the kitchen the hall door opened again and Felice came edging through it, turning the bottom of her stocking cap down over her ears. "I'm coming too," she told me. "I just want to watch his face and see if he's pleased."

In a couple of minutes me and my broom were stirring up a blizzard while my face turned numb and the insides of my nostrils tried to stick shut permanently. I worked at top speed to keep warm and was careful only around the crucial spot where I'd taken the box off Felice's handiwork. Finally I swept my way up to the front door and was reaching for the button when the inside door opened and there he was—business suit, sad little smile, and all. He unlatched the storm door. "Come in, Timmie, come in! The world's fastest sweeper shouldn't have to stand on the doorstep in weather like this. But you shouldn't have come so early. This afternoon it should be at least a little warmer."

"Well, I said I would," I told him, "and anyway, there's something I want to show you. If you could spare a couple of minutes—it's right outside."

He hesitated, looking bewildered, and who could blame him. I said, "Please, Mr. Weinstock, it's . . . it's *important*."

It took him only a second to make up his mind. "Of course," he said, turning toward the front hall closet to the right of the door.

"Mr. Weinstock," I began. This was my big moment. Tie game, two men on, bottom of the ninth, and me stepping into the batter's box. And all of a sudden I didn't know what I was supposed to do. Catch the ball? Kick the umpire? Sing the Star-Spangled Banner? "It's . . . a kind of a surprise," I said feebly.

He was already shrugging into his overcoat. "Surprises I like, Timmie." He reached to the closet shelf and brought down a dark gray fedora and settled it firmly on his head. "Now. You lead, I follow."

Starting down the front steps, I began to get stage fright. What if he wouldn't want a gaudy thing like that in front of his house and would be too kindhearted to say so?

Before you could say electric chair we had arrived

and were looking down at Felice's work of art. Mr. Weinstock stood beside me, still as a stone. He went on looking at it for what seemed a couple of whole minutes and he didn't say a word, long enough anyway so that I couldn't stand it, had to put an end to that awful silence. So I babbled. "I didn't draw it," I said. "My sister did. She's an artist. But it was my idea. But it's only chalk, so if you don't like it I can clean it off easy. Underneath it's clean as a bedsheet, all the black paint is gone. I used a wire brush and . . ."

Right then I heard a queer stopped-up kind of sound and looked up to see that his eyes were wet. Could have been the cold. Still he didn't say anything but reached out and grabbed my shoulder hard enough to hurt if I hadn't been padded by about three layers of wool. And he went on doing it, like he didn't want to let go.

I felt all mixed up—terrible and good and glad and sad and I knew I had to get away from there before . . . before I did something really stupid. I said, "Gotta go," and headed for home fast. But right at the corner of the hedge I turned around and got out a few more words. "Happy New Year!" I said. It wasn't New Year's yet, but it sure was celebration time. Mr. Weinstock still didn't say anything but raised one hand and waved it, looking toward me, and waved again, and I took off.

I'd glimpsed Felice's colorful sweater through the hedge, and now we arrived at the side door in a dead heat, plunged in out of the cold and stood there a while before starting to shed sweaters and things. For reasons I couldn't figure out we were both grinning like jack-o'-lanterns. I said, "Well, I guess he liked it."

"*Liked* it! He was *overwhelmed. Stunned.* He was *dumbfounded!*"

Grinning some more, I said, "Yeah, I guess he was."

Speaking through a sweater that was halfway off, she said, "You didn't need to tell him I drew it—but it was pretty nice of you."

I said, "For gosh sakes, I wasn't about to pretend I did it. Nobody in his right mind would believe it."

Anyway, it didn't matter. I already felt so swelled up I needed a new skin to hold me. Whatever else might happen between now and May Day I'd have done one thing right.

CHAPTER
7

The Elbow of Fate

NOT UNTIL I'D gone upstairs and crossed "Mr. Weinstock" off my list—feeling solemn, as if I'd made
history—did I remember what this cold wave really
meant to me. About six seconds later I was downstairs
looking at the mantel clock, which said it was twenty
minutes to nine. At the stroke of nine I was on the
phone giving Central the number of the city parks
department.

On about the sixth ring a lady answered, sounding a
little breathless. I asked if the ponds were open for
skating and after a few seconds she said, "Are you
standing there with your mittens on and your skates in
your hand?"

I told her I hadn't got quite that far. She said, "Tell
you what. Give me ten minutes to take my hat off and
find out what's going on around here. Then call back."

I gave her my name, so she'd know it was me,
allowed her thirteen minutes, then phoned. "This
Tim?" she said before I could even open my mouth.

"Yes, ma'am."

"Bad news, Tim. Nothing open yet. What part of town you live in?"

I told her and she said, "Well, you can count on Waveland tomorrow morning, ten o'clock, if this weather holds. Today I guess you'll just have to stay home and help your mother."

Deciding that the best way to help my mother was to stay out of her way, I went over to Ed's and gave him the news about Waveland. We agreed to get there as close to ten o'clock as we could, taking the streetcar to the end of the line and walking from there.

It was hard to just sit around and talk about skating when we wanted to go right that minute, but one way or another we managed to put in the time, keeping an eye out for the snow that might or might not come. And all that afternoon and on through the night those mighty forces of fate, soundless and invisible, kept laboring on, making everything ready for tomorrow and Carl Simons's meeting, arranging the lives of certain people, strangers to me, so that they too would be on that ice at the proper time, all playing their parts in the grand scheme.

If I'd known how important I was I might have enjoyed it more.

When we got to Waveland Park golf course they had a fire going already on the north side of the pond and there were big logs around to sit on while you put on your skates. There were a dozen or so people on the ice—kids and grown-ups both—and more getting ready. It struck me as a real pretty scene—just like the picture in my mind when I'd first got my skates. But I was in too much of a hurry to sit around enjoying the scenery. I was ready before Ed was and I got up and went to the edge of the ice on my blade points so as to keep from dulling the whole length. Then I was on the ice, pushing off into a glide, and—*wow*—it was like flying! Compared with the old clamp-ons, the new skates made me feel like what's-his-name with the winged sandals. Those old skates were the tin lizzies and these were the Duesenbergs. They made me feel like there was nothing I couldn't do and I took off like the wind—jigging, zigzagging, figure-eights, stopping on a dime, forgetting my list and everything else. All I wanted to do was enjoy the winter's first day of skating. It had been a long, long wait. And when this winter's ice melted there'd be a still longer wait. Like forever.

When I rang the doorbell at the Simons' house on Thursday, an eight- or nine-year-old girl—Carl's sister no doubt—let me in. She stared wide-eyed, which wasn't surprising since for the last three hours or so my right eye had been looking like a stomped-on stewed prune. The first shiner of my life. She didn't say anything at first, but finally pointed toward a room beyond the living room and mumbled, "They're in there." Then she remembered what else she was supposed to do and added, "You can lay your things on the sofa like the rest of 'em did."

I followed instructions, then headed for that other room where I could hear voices. I took a couple of deep breaths to steady myself and stepped through the door. First there was dead silence, then a minor uproar. Carl led it. "Holy Moses! What's the other guy look like?"

I was ready for that one, having had time to

rehearse. "Don't know," I said. "He's in the hospital." It got a laugh. The only one who refrained was Judy. She was sitting in a wide-backed white wicker chair that must have been made to show her off. She'd clapped a hand to her mouth the instant I appeared, as if it was a terrible shock. Now she removed it and said, "Timmy—how awful! Your eye must hurt like *fury*."

"Nothing I can't stand," I said. Pain meant nothing to the likes of me.

I had it figured right: Fate had given me a black eye in a good cause. Right off I'd got Judy's attention and she was loaded with sympathy.

I looked into those terrific eyes until unconsciousness threatened. What saved me was Liza Greene, a girl who runs more to funny than pretty. In her usual explosive way, she said, "Well, speak up! Tell all! You can't expect us to sit here and look at that . . . that *thing* . . . and not know!"

Carl pointed to a chair and said, "She's right. Sit down, take a load off your eye—end the suspense."

I sat. Unfortunately the chair was next to his, not Judy's, but you can't have everything. Right there my luck ran out, or so it seemed. I had the floor and the audience but a lousy speech. In a flash I thought of several dramatic ways I could have got a black eye other than the way I did, but I knew I'd never get away with any of them. I remembered Uncle Art's version of an old saying. "Honesty is the best policy because if you lie you'll get caught." He claimed Moses said that.

What I said was, "The truth is it was just a dumb accident. A friend and I went skating out at Waveland, right after lunch. There was this high-school guy showing off what a flash he was on the ice. Top speed, backwards, forwards—every which way. I saw him miss half a dozen people by a hair."

"Boy, do I know that type!" said Carl.

There was a groaned chorus of "Me too!"

"Well, I was the one he *didn't* miss. Crashed into me full-tilt going backwards. Caught me in the eye with his elbow, and I hit the ice like a bag of cement."

Somebody said, "Ouch!" with feeling.

"I think I used a better word," I said, and added, "My mother made me hold raw meat on the thing for an hour. Slowed down the swelling but didn't do much for the looks of it."

Actually, it was during that hour that my great idea came to me for the *Highlight*.

As I'd expected, it all sounded as flat as yesterday's root beer, so it was a relief when Carl said it was time to get down to business. I figured I'd used up most of my time in the spotlight, although everybody kept glancing at my eye now and then. It was one of those things you keep peeking at just because you know it's there—like a hole in somebody's pants.

There was still some spotlight time, though. With Fate on your side it's hard to go wrong. I listened to the ideas the others put forth and sloshed them around in my mind, like mouthwash, and honestly couldn't help thinking mine was better. Finally Carl turned to me and said, "Tim, we'd like to hear from you too."

I let that hang in the air until people had time to think, "What's this dummy here for, the refreshments?" Then I said, with Modesty printed all over me in capital letters, "Well, I did have a kind of a brainstorm."

I hadn't planned my speech. Just played it by ear. "Everybody," I began, "likes to see his name in print." Without really looking I could see heads nodding and I pushed on. "Particularly if his name's on top of something he wrote." More nods. "*Especially* if there's a picture of him along with it."

I risked a quick look at Judy and found her eyes fixed on me, lips parted a little, as if I'd been John Barrymore or Rudolph Valentino. Or Laurel and Hardy? I took in an extra supply of air and got to the point. "Why couldn't we sponsor a literary competition? Anybody in school who's written a story or a poem, essay, or anything—and I bet there's a lot more than you'd think—is invited to enter the contest. We'll name a judging committee, and the winning poems and things will be published with those little half-column photos set into the type a couple of inches below the authors' names. Publication will be the prize and . . . and I guess that's it."

Well, they didn't sing "For He's a Jolly Good Fellow" or carry me around the room on their shoulders, but the reaction was more than I could have hoped for: stirrings, mutterings, quick little conferences neighbor-to-neighbor, and finally—sweet music—exclamations such as "Hey, Tim, nice going!" "Swell idea!" and "Just decided *my* idea stinks!"

The modesty expression was starting to cramp my face when Carl spoke up. "Sounds to me like we've got a unanimous decision here, but if anybody's got a different idea now's the time we should hear it."

Silence, beautiful silence. Carl cocked his head and put a hand behind his ear and frowned as if he thought he'd gone deaf, and finally said, "Well, folks, looks like this meeting has come to the fastest decision on record."

"Oh drat!" Liza blurted. "You mean we've got to go home before the refreshments?"

Carl shook his head. "We're not adjourning yet! Plenty of details to iron out! Like who's going to be the judges." He opened a little notebook. "So come on with the questions, suggestions, or whatever's on your minds."

The meeting got noisy then, Carl scribbled away in the notebook, and the time went by so fast we were startled when Carl's mother and little sister came in and began handing out little paper plates, cookies, and paper cups full of cider. My cup was already running over, so to speak, but even geniuses enjoy food and drink, and while I was consuming my share I concentrated on watching Judy through the slit in my bad eye while appearing to look elsewhere with the good one. It didn't work very well and I gave it up after realizing I was screwing my face up in a way that probably looked like I'd eaten something rotten.

The gathering had to break up sometime and was in the process when I had yet another brilliant idea, and I was inclined to take credit for this one myself, Fate already having done everything I could expect from it.

Everybody was milling around in the front room, thanking Mrs. Simons for the cookies and hospitality and putting on coats and things. I asked to use the phone and when I called home Uncle Art answered. He said, "If it's a chauffeur you want, sport, I'm your man."

I'd no more than hung up than there was Judy right at my elbow. "My turn," she said, reaching for the phone. I asked, "You calling home for a ride?" When she nodded I spoke fast. "My uncle's coming for me and he'd be glad to drop you at home on the way. No need to bother your folks."

She dimpled up. "How do you know it's on the way?"

Fast thinking required here. I couldn't very well admit I'd known her address for years. Looked it up in the phone book. But I wasn't through being brilliant yet. "Anywhere you want to go," I said, "is on the way."

Uh oh, I thought. Went too far that time. Sounded more like Uncle Art than me. But she just laughed, treating me to another look at the dimples. "Maybe your uncle won't feel that way about it."

"He will," I said. "He's not just my uncle, he's my friend."

I didn't really know how good a friend until we went out to get in the car. He'd brought my folks' Oakland sedan instead of his own Model T. Warmer—and classier. Uncle Art leaned over and swung the door open for us. "Pile in here with me, kids; we'll all keep warmer that way." If that was the case Judy must have been the warmest of all because she was jammed between the two of us. As for me, I'd have been warm if it was eighty below. The side of me next to her felt like it was up against a stove.

It turned out not to be far out of the way at all—not

nearly far enough to suit me. Uncle Art drove up in her driveway. I got out and helped her out, doing it about as gracefully as a horse would, I think. She said, "Thanks a million, Uncle Art," then laughed, sounding like little bells on a Christmas package, and added, "I'm sorry, but that's all I know to call you."

He said, "Generations of kids have called me Uncle Art. It was a treat to meet you, Judy."

To me she said, "See you when vacation's over, Timmie. Take care of that eye now!"

Take care of it! What I wanted to do was pickle it or something so it would last a while. My first black eye had brought me more good luck than all the four-leaf clovers I'd found so far in my whole life.

I said, "See you, Judy. See you soon." And I thought, *This can't last.* Tongue-tied Tim can't be gone forever!

On the way home Uncle Art said, "That's some sweet girl there, Tim."

I grabbed my chance. "Well, she's the reason I've been looking for the right time to ask you for, you know, a few pointers on how to—"

He interrupted. "Hold on, sport! It doesn't look like you need any help from me. Whatever you've been doing, just keep on with it."

That night in bed I couldn't help asking myself over and over: Can they really be right, those people saying the world will end? It *can't* end, I kept thinking. Not *now*!

CHAPTER

8

Happy New Year!

THE NEXT DAY was New Year's Eve. Tomorrow, 1928, the first year ever with only four months in it.

Suddenly May Day seemed an awful lot closer than it had the day before—and I was hardly more than *started* on the program I'd set for myself. It wasn't just time I needed, either, but luck. No matter how hard I worked at everything I'd still need more luck than the Man Who Broke the Bank at Monte Carlo.

The luck I got that day wasn't the kind I was looking for.

I went down to the Y in the middle of the morning, taking along some of my snow-shoveling money so I could eat lunch at the Y cafeteria in case I wasn't ready to come home at lunchtime.

I found a guy to play a couple games of pingpong with, then went swimming and got into a wild game of water polo, which took my mind clear off the end of the world and all the things I had to do before it happened.

This carefree state of mind lasted as long as it took me to shower, get dressed, and head up the stairs on my way to the cafeteria. At the top of the stairs I barely missed running head-on into a guy who was starting down.

Dunk Bolander.

He didn't get out of my way, which was no surprise, so there we were, face to face, and my morning was ruined. He put on the sneer that he pretends is a smile and looked me over. First thing to catch his eye, naturally, was my shiner, which hadn't got any less spectacular overnight. "Well, mercy sakes alive, just looky *you*! Some great big nasty boy get *mean* to you?"

I grabbed in all directions for a way out of this. But the only way was backwards, down the stairs, and I just couldn't do that, no matter what happened. "He was nasty," I said, "but he wasn't big, except for his mouth."

He turned the sneer into a snarl. "You lookin' for trouble?"

While he snarled I heard voices from the hall behind him. People coming. "No," I said, "just looking for the way out of here. You planning to move?"

"You plannin' to *make* me?"

Well, now or never. It wasn't courage, just desperation. I crouched a little and lunged forwards, slamming both hands against his chest.

Caught off balance, he staggered backwards. Fate was still on my side. The instant this happened the two guys whose voices I'd heard rounded the corner from the hall and Dunk banged into both of them. They were about eighteen and a lot bigger than us.

Dunk acted as if they weren't even there, going instantly into a fighter's crouch instead, fists up and ready. I did the same, knowing it wasn't going to do me a bit of good.

Fate decided to referee. One of the big guys moved suddenly, wrapping his arms around Dunk, pinning him. "Try using your *brains*, you kids!" he said, his voice jerky because Dunk was struggling to get loose. The other big guy took it from there. "If you gotta fight, go out in the street. Do it in here and you get kicked out."

Dunk had stopped struggling now and the first guy spoke again. "Okay. If I let go of you will you go outside?"

"Or stay here," put in his friend, "and shake hands and forget about whatever's eatin' on you. Get smart."

"Ain't gonna shake hands," Dunk said, yanking out the sleeves of his sweatshirt where the guy had grabbed him.

"Me either," I said. Getting reckless.

"Ain't gonna go outside neither." Dunk was talking to me, not them, and slowly he replaced his murderous glare with the familiar sneer, which had a sort of crafty look this time. "What I'm gonna do is I'm gonna wait till you're finished with all them pewgilism lessons. Then we'll find out if they've did you any good—unless you leave town first."

So he knew I was signed up for the January seventh class. He must have been keeping closer track of me than I had any idea. I said, with teeth gritted, "I'll be around."

Now that I knew I wasn't going to get flattened, there was just no holding me back.

"By that time," one of the big guys said,"you won't even remember what to fight about."

I went on up to the cafeteria, wondering if I might be too stirred up to eat much of anything. But I recovered in short order and managed to get my thirty-five cents worth and a little more.

During the afternoon Ed came over. Naturally I told him the whole story and he was about as full of admiration as I'd thought he'd be. "I've never seen the guy," he said, "but if he's half as tough as you say he is it strikes me you pushed your luck a lot further than you pushed him."

"You might have something there," I said, "but at least I didn't fold up the way I've been doing."

"You could call that progress," he said, "but what I'm wondering is what you'd've done if the big guys hadn't showed up just when they did."

"Maybe I'd've found out how I looked with a broken jaw *and* a black eye," I said. Then I changed the subject. "What do you say we take another crack at hitching tonight? Catch a ride or two? Unless you're gun-shy after last time."

Ed flared up. "What makes you think I'm any more gun-shy than you? I'd go like a shot, only I can't."

"Why not?"

"Simple. My folks are going to a New Year's party and I've got to stay home with my sister."

"What the heck for? Nothing's going to happen to her right in her own house!"

"Tell that to my dad. Or my *sister*. She's scared of burglars and bogeymen and anything else she can think of."

We agreed to try again when street conditions got

better than they were now and Ed went home saying he was going to try a little prayer and meditation to get in shape to spend an entire evening and maybe half the night with nobody to talk to but his sister.

I told him if things got too bad he could phone me and I'd tell him about what a great fighter I was going to be. He said that on second thought his sister, Ellen, was really a great conversationalist once she got going.

With Ed around it's impossible for anyone else to get the last word in.

After he left, the house seemed pretty quiet except for an occasional snatch of conversation between Felice and my mother. Felice was taking a bath, so they talked through the bathroom door, which meant I could hear my mother plainly enough but Felice hardly at all. Things like, "Yes, you may use some, providing you don't slosh it all over yourself like it was rainwater. It doesn't come from the dime store, you know."

And a minute later: "No, definitely not. A hat wouldn't be suitable at all. It's a girls' party, remember, not dinner at the White House!"

I got my current library book and settled down in my father's easy chair. That is, I tried to settle down. It was a good book, called *Scaramouche*. Plenty of excitement, and it would have grabbed me right off if another subject hadn't grabbed first. Judy Felton. Why didn't I just call her up and, well, chat?

Chat? Me? I'd never chatted in my life.

Well, why not? Other kids did it all the time.

But what would I say? "Hi, Judy. Wait'll I tell you: I almost got in a fight this morning. Boy, was I scared! What've *you* been doing?"

Well, I could talk about *Highlight* stuff, couldn't I?

ME: Hi, Judy, this is Tim.

JUDY: Tim who?

ME: Ha ha. Uh, I was just wondering how we'd organize things when the contest stuff starts coming in. . . .

But that was a *subject*. Chatting was supposed to be sort of aimless and empty-headed. Well, maybe you could start with a subject and get empty-headed as you went along.

I dithered around like this for at least five minutes, maybe ten, finally surged to my feet, all resolute and dauntless, marched into the breakfast room where the phone is, and gave Central Judy's number. The instant I did it cowardice took hold and told me not to worry; I could hang up before the phone rang, or even when somebody answered. With any luck, nobody was home anyway.

I was still prospecting for more possibilities when there was a click and a voice—*the* voice—said, "Felton residence, Judy speaking." I might've known, even her manners were beautiful.

Sounding like a frog with bronchitis, I said, "Uh, hi, Judy, this is Tim."

"Oh." Pause. "Oh hello, Tim." I wondered who she'd been expecting. And why didn't *she* start chatting? After all, she was a cinch to know how. The silence went on long enough to recite "Hiawatha." Finally desperation loosened my cork and I blurted something about when the contest entries started coming in maybe we could meet in the gym or somewhere and maybe read a couple to each other, or if she didn't like that idea we might— It was a vast relief when she broke in on that sentence, which I couldn't find any way out of.

"Oh Timmie, I'm terribly sorry, but could you call me another time, maybe tomorrow? Right now I'm so busy I can't see straight. I'm going to this New Year's party, and I just now found out my dress needs altering. My mother's working like fury on it, and then I'll have to press it and—oh, a dozen things!"

Stumbling all over myself I told her not to worry about it, that I'd talk to her another time, that I hoped she'd have a real great time at the party, and even remembered to wish her a happy new year, which I thought was pretty chivalrous under the circumstances. Then I went back to the easy chair and did my best to get lost in the adventures of Scaramouche. But it didn't work; I couldn't concentrate on the words because of the broken record in my head that kept repeating every word I'd spoken into the telephone. In that brief little chat I'd found out just about where I stood with Judy Felton. If a cow came around maybe I could get up the nerve to kiss *it*.

The way this day was turning out, I'd have been better off getting beat up by Dunk Bolander.

I kept on trying to read, comprehending about every other sentence, until finally my mother called me to come set the table for dinner. This didn't do anything to turn me bright and cheery, so I called back, "Well, *why*, for gosh sake? It's Felice's turn!"

"She's busy getting ready for her party!"

"She's *been* getting ready all day!"

"Timothy, come in here please!"

Uh oh. I knew that tone of voice, so I did what she

said. When I came in she was lighting the gas in the oven. "I don't care to argue at the top of my voice. Anyway, there's no argument. I'm asking you to set the table and I'll see to it that Felice takes your turn next time you fail to show up on schedule—which probably won't be far away. There will be six at the table."

I wanted to ask how come there'd be six if Felice wouldn't be there but thought better of it, which was a good thing because in a minute I remembered Grampa was coming in off the road for the weekend. I kept my mouth shut and set the table.

Dinnertime turned out to be pretty lively. For one thing Felice kept jackrabbiting down the stairs and through the kitchen to the phone where she'd talk in a low voice. Her party was an all-night blast for a whole slew of girls. I guessed the night wouldn't last long enough to get all the necessary talking done.

Grampa had some funny stories he'd picked up from his customers. That reminded Uncle Art of a couple of his own and then Grampa said, "It was a long ways from funny up in Mason City on Tuesday—no, Wednesday. I like to wore myself out and froze besides."

"How come?" my father prompted.

"Whole dang town was taken over by a crowd of them end-of-the-world fanatics. A thousand of 'em, by the look of it. They filled up all the parking places downtown while they had their big shindig in the Legion Hall. I had to get to my customers on foot, carrying my sample bags. Umpteen below and all them jackasses inside and warm, singin' and carryin' on and—"

I saw my father look across the table at my mother, then cut his eyes toward me for a split second, and then he interrupted, smooth as silk. "Better tone it down, Dad, you never know whose toes you might be stepping on."

"Huh?" Grampa said, looking startled, added "Oh!" and humphed into his napkin, then stirred his coffee like it was red hot, which it couldn't have been.

Now my father said, "Come to think of it, there was a pretty good one making the rounds at the office. There was this fellow—out west somewhere—who went into the drugstore and asked for forty bottles of something the druggist couldn't understand. And . . ."

I can't remember anything else about the joke except that it was funny and everybody laughed including Grampa and we all let sleeping dogs lie and got through dinner in good shape.

My fellow slave at the kitchen sink that evening was Aunt Lizzie, who had volunteered. Ordinarily it's understood that she's excused from housework because she's a paying boarder with work of her own to do—correcting papers, getting assignments ready, teacher stuff. But she said she wanted to make sure Felice got off to her party on time so that the phone would quit ringing. I said if I'd known it would work I'd have got myself invited to a party too. Aunt Lizzie said, "Maybe it's not too late. Ask your uncle if you can go to *his*."

My mother said, "Over my dead body!" and Uncle Art gave me a big wink.

While my aunt and I labored, Felice, with a lot of

yelling down the stairs to my mother, finished getting herself gussied up for the party. She stuffed a little suitcase with enough gear to take her to Argentina and back, and while my father was getting the car out to take her my mother loaded her up with an encyclopedia's worth of rules about what a young lady should do and not do as a guest in somebody's home.

After all the excitement died down and the dishes were done and put away, I wandered up to Uncle Art's room. He already had his starched shirt on and the tux pants with the silky black stripes down the sides and was sitting on the edge of his bed sliding his patent-leather shoes out of the socklike wool covers they wore between parties.

He didn't look up, just peered at a shoe, rubbed it with the sock thing, peered again, then breathed on it and rubbed what might or might not have been a smudge. I couldn't see any smudges but I could see the soles were about the thickness of cardboard. I said, "You planning to wear those things in the snow? You'll probably fall on your can."

He looked up as if it was a big surprise to see me, then put the gleaming shoes on and tied the laces. Finally he said, "Where I'm going they clear the walks three times a day if they have to."

"Where's that?" I said.

"Church."

"Church!" I said. "You going to get married?"

"I *hope* not. It's choir practice."

I knew he was just stringing me along, so I plopped down on his easy chair and prepared to enjoy it. I said, "You going to sing hymns and drink booze too?"

He stood up and started to tie the black bow tie in the mirror that hangs above his chest of drawers. "Not at the same time," he said.

Pretty soon I said, "Your girl, she sing in the choir too?"

"Not a note. Poor thing's tone deaf."

"I bet she can sure dance the night away though."

He stepped to the closet, got out his tux jacket, shrugged it into the right shape, and studied it front and back. Then he flipped a small whiskbroom from the dresser top to me. I caught it automatically and he said, "Make yourself useful."

While I imitated a barbershop porter whisking away bits of lint from the tux he said, "How old are you now—thirteen?"

"Closer to fourteen."

He nodded, looking resigned, and said, "One of these days you and I had better have a looong talk." With a flourish he snaked from its drawer a silky white scarf and draped it around his neck, gave it an approving look, and flipped me a semi-salute. "Time's a-wastin'," he said. "Turn off the light when you get around to it." He strode down the hall toward the stairs.

I followed him down to listen to my mother praise his looks and his getup. In the middle of it a car horn hooted from the drive and Uncle Art said, "There's my driver!" While he put on his black topcoat and organized the scarf under it my mother said, "I do hope he's a *good* driver."

"Trained him myself," Uncle Art said, putting his arm around her and squeezing. "Don't you worry, Sis, I'm a growed-up man now."

My father, who had just got back from taking Felice to her party, said, "Enjoy yourself, Art—but not too much. And if you get arrested don't call me; I can wait and read about it in the paper."

When he was gone we all sort of looked sideways at each other and finally Aunt Lizzie said, "It's always been this way. When Arthur leaves a room it seems . . . *depopulated*."

It wasn't hard to see what she meant. I began to feel sort of left out, with Felice and Uncle Art off to parties. Not to mention Judy Felton. This was dumb because I didn't think I'd even *like* New Year's Eve parties. All I'd heard about or seen in the movies convinced me that all people did was dance and drink until they got noisy, and eat little tiny sandwiches with the crusts cut off, then someone would pass out silly paper hats and noisemakers, and at the stroke of midnight they'd yell and scream and wave champagne glasses around and sing "Auld Lang Syne" way off key and everybody kiss each other. Nobody was going to invite me to that kind of party anyway, so there was no point in thinking about it.

My mother said I could stay up till midnight and listen to the new year come in on the radio, or step outside and listen to the racket of car horns and party horns and people whooping it up all around. I thought about it but since it wasn't going to be much of a year anyway, I wasn't in a sweat to stay up and greet it. Besides, I was getting sleepy already and it was only about 9:30.

I read my book awhile and the others tried playing a game of three-handed bridge which, from the things they said, I figured was about as interesting as oatmeal without cream. After a while they gave up and headed upstairs, all except my father who said he'd stay up a spell and get started on a report he'd brought home from the office.

I went up, got undressed, and went to bed. I lay there and listened to the wind whooshing through the bare branches of the big birch tree outside and batting now and then at the underside of the eaves. It wasn't a big wind, so I could ignore it. What I couldn't ignore was my imagination, which was up and dressed and ready for action. The wind was all the encouragement it needed, and in no time at all I was working out yet *another* way the world could end—and it was a scary one.

On the first of May, with no warning at all, God would stop the planet's rotation. *Whop*—like that! But He wouldn't bother about the law of momentum, so the atmosphere would keep right on going, and it would seem to anybody who lived long enough to think about it that a monstrous, unimaginably gigantic wind was blowing. At hundreds of miles a minute, faster than all the hurricanes of history, it would fling all living things around like dust in a vacuum sweeper and flatten every structure standing—power poles and their lines, houses, bridges, windmills, buildings, everything. Nothing living would escape, not even men in mines and moles in their burrows, because with the wind would come the water. The instant the earth stopped, every ocean, lake, and river would slop out over cities, deserts, farmland, and all but the tops of the highest mountains.

The force of that vast tidal wave crashing down on everything in its way not only would make the greatest noise ever heard but would set the earth to trembling and shaking in a series of mighty earthquakes. . . .

At some point things got muddled. I was rolling with the spasms of the earth and the quake was speaking in a human voice, a hoarse whisper, and it knew my name. "Timmie . . . come on . . . wake up. Wake up!"

I opened my eyes, sort of, and my father stopped shaking the corner of my bed. Grinning, he said, "*Finally*! My next move would have been to call the undertaker. Look, it's a quarter to midnight. Thought you might like to join me in a quiet, exclusive celebration. Just you and me. I stocked up on ice cream and soda pop, just in case. Nobody's touched it." That got my attention, and lord knows I was glad to get out of that dream. I got up.

The floor was solid and unmoving. No quake, no hurricane, no monstrous flood.

We made it down the hall, down the stairs, and through the little hall between the stair landing and the kitchen without a sound except our breathing. He told me to go turn on the little lamp on the breakfast table. I could see the sense in that because the window was high in the wall and the lamplight wouldn't light up the snow outside the way the bright kitchen light would.

I did it and he said, "Make like a burglar and get the ice cream scoop out of the drawer without making a sound. Then do the same with a couple of those yellow bowls. Spoons too."

I followed orders while he went to the ice box on the back porch. There's something about sneaking around in a dark house where people are asleep that makes things a lot more exciting than they have any good reason to be, and while I put the things on the table he set down a quart carton of maple-nut ice cream and a quart bottle of ginger ale. "Think this'll do?" he asked and I used a slurping noise to express my opinion.

From his bathrobe pocket he pulled out his watch and chain and peered at the watch. "Two minutes to 1928," he said with satisfaction, switching from a whisper to a low tone. "Just right!" Then he looped the watchchain over a hook in the archway between the kitchen and breakfast room. The hook used to hold a little basket thing with a plant in it until my father bumped his head on it once too often. Now he took a sighting along the wall and set the watch to swinging at the end of the chain like a pendulum. "My guess is it'll swing till next year." We both stared a few seconds at the feeble lamplight glinting on the gold of the chain and watch. "I'll dish up the ice cream," he said. "You open the bottle."

When that was done we sat down facing each other and I picked up my spoon. He stopped me with a little shake of the head. "Stroke of midnight."

We watched, halfway hypnotized it seemed to me, while that circle of gold swung left, swung right, each swing a fraction shorter than the one before, each swing marking off a piece of a second in the little time left in the year we were about to say good-bye to.

The way I felt seemed impossible — chilly but at the same time sort of warm, like having a fire in the fireplace on a cold morning. The chilly part was the thought of saying good-bye to the last complete year there would ever be and hello to the one that was scheduled to be chopped short on a pretty spring day. The warm part was being here at this table, the only person invited to my father's secret New Year's Eve party, watching the gleaming gold disk swing to ever lower levels. There surely couldn't be more than thirty seconds to go now.

That brought an urgent worry to me and I broke what was getting to be a tense silence. "From here we can't see the face of the watch, so we won't know—"

"We'll know," he said. "We'll *hear* the new year come."

Well, how dumb could I get! Naturally we'd hear it. Right now, all over the city, people had their eyes glued to timepieces of all sorts, or to their radios as if they could *see* the man who was dramatically counting the seconds backwards from ten, or twenty, or whatever. They'd be clutching tin horns, whistles, and those ratchety-clatter things that make a noise like a stick along a picket fence. . . .

Now the watch was swinging only a quarter-inch or so to either side. My father said, "Get ready!"

I looked at him and he looked as excited as I felt. I didn't know whether he was catching the excitement from me or the other way around. He startled me then by sort of flowing to his feet and crossing the space between him and the watch, now barely moving, and taking it in his hand. One quick look . . . "Pour!"

The word was like a signal to the world. Car horns blared and blatted, voices were raised—thin and far off—firecrackers rackety-popped, engine drivers 'way over in the railyards on the east side yanked the lanyards on their steam whistles. Nearby it would have drilled you from ear to ear; here it was a mournful muted wail from Never-Never Land. I tipped the bottle into my glass and the carbonation made a foam that threatened to rise to the rim and overflow. My first thoughts in 1928 were, first,that I was going to mess up the table and, second, a hope that all the racket came from far enough away that it wouldn't wake my mother who'd find my father missing and come down to see what he was up to. It was mean of me, and selfish, but I couldn't help feeling that this time, this funny little celebration belonged to my father and me and couldn't be shared with anyone else, not even her.

Right away he put an end to my shameful line of thinking. "Tell you what," he said in his loud whisper. "We can't do anything noisy, so let's salute the new year with a handshake." He put his hand out, and after a couple of seconds I grabbed it and we shook.

His grip was hard and I hardened mine all I could. We looked at each other. The rule is, you've got to when you shake hands. I didn't say anything. Couldn't. Then he let go and said, "Pour me some champagne and we'll drink a toast. It's one of the requirements."

I filled his glass without running it over and he lifted it up. "What'll we drink to? You name it."

"To . . . to . . ." I stuttered because I'd never proposed a toast. I'd read plenty of them, but they always said something like "Confusion to the French!" or "God save His Majesty the King!" I finally mumbled feebly, "To the new year—I guess."

That wasn't exactly resounding and I was relieved when my father said, "Maybe I've got a better one.

What say we drink . . ." He put a little pause in there. "To the Waldens!"

"To the Waldens!" I said, hearing my voice get a little too loud. We clinked glasses. So there was the first toast in my life—and maybe the last, although for once I didn't think about that—drunk with Clicquot Club ginger ale. The little bubbles fizzed up in my throat and rose on up to somewhere in back of my nose and made my eyes water. Then we dug into the ice cream. The racket outside didn't last very long and after it died down my father eased off a little on making ice cream disappear and said, "We drank our toast to the Waldens, and that of course includes Grampa."

I lowered my spoon which was on its way up with a load and said, "Well, uh, *sure*," and tensed up a little, wondering where this was heading.

"Your grandfather," he went on, "is a good man, a fine man, but tactfulness is not one of his virtues. Never has been. He speaks his mind freely—often too freely—without considering the effect on those who don't share his views." He took another spoonful and swallowed. "I'm bringing this up because I'd hate to think his dinnertime remarks may affect the way you feel about him."

I opened my mouth to answer but he held up his hand. "One more thing. I've already spoken to your mother about this and she understands that Grampa does not believe either she *or* you is a jackass or a fanatic, that if he'd known your views about the world's end he'd never—"

I couldn't help breaking in. "Gosh, all I thought was, 'That's just Grampa.' Anyway, I know there are plenty of people who think just the same as he does. Even Ed Guthrie makes whole speeches along that line, and he's still my best friend!"

My father smiled, looking relieved, and went at the ice cream where he'd left off. In a minute he said, "Well, I should have known. For your age you're pretty levelheaded."

I looked down at my bowl a lot more modestly than I was feeling, and he proceeded to make modesty even more difficult. "Another thing," he said, "while we're on the subject. I've got to hand it to you for sticking to what you believe whether I, or Ed Guthrie, or anyone else, disagrees with you. Takes guts."

I mumbled "Gee, thanks" and made a big job of scraping the melted ice cream from the bottom of my bowl, but I couldn't feel comfortable with the compliment. If I had guts, why did I spend most of my time feeling scared? I thought about all those mobs of people in the newspaper stories and pictures. Were they all as scared as I was, or did they have some other reason for getting on this bandwagon—hundreds or thousands more every day?

Here in this kitchen where I'd spent maybe half my life, with the first minutes of the final year ticking away, it seemed like the best and maybe the only time I'd ever get to ask what my father thought about these questions that were so much too big for me. So I asked him why he thought so many thousands were flocking . to join the end-of-the-world people.

He went on scraping for so long without saying anything that I wondered if he hadn't heard me or if I hadn't really said anything. Finally, still eyeing the bowl and scraping away, he said, "You're well past the age when a boy believes his old dad knows all there is to know, but you deserve an answer to your question, and I'll give it my best effort."

Now he stopped spooning and looked up at me. "I lay a big part of it to one of the oddities of the human animal: we're fascinated by death and bloodshed and disaster. And the end of the world would be the biggest imaginable disaster. Think about it. If there's a murder and we don't get to look at the body we gawk at the spot where it bled into the street. If there's an explosion we have to be blocked off by the police to keep us from getting under the feet of the rescuers. We follow the fire engines in the hope of seeing houses burnt to the ground and people jumping out of windows.

"We invented gladitorial fights, and all the blood sports—fighting cocks, dog against dog, dogs against bears or bulls. And best of all, war. A movie war will do if we haven't got the real thing. We don't usually admit it, but we're excited by violence and death and destruction. I remember the recruiting depots in the big war when you were just a baby. Young men stood for hours in long lines to sign up. They called it patriotism but actually the whole idea was more exciting than anything they'd ever known and they were afraid they'd miss the fun. It was a kind of hysteria, and in a lot of ways the end of the world is like that. Death and destruction carried as far as they'll go."

He reached for my bowl, put it inside his own and the spoons inside that. But he wasn't through talking yet. "Don't get me wrong; I don't say all this is true of everyone who believes the end is near. There's a central core of honest believers—like your mother, and probably yourself. They're convinced by the teaching of their leaders. But as more come to believe, and their views are spread by the press, the radio, word of mouth, the fascination sets in, the hysteria, and more and more people *want* to believe. War is frightening but fascinating all the same. This is more so because it's unknown. Never happened before, and maybe won't this time."

He stood up, carried the bowls to the sink, then turned. "And at this point the whole shebang merges with another oddity of the human animal: We *enjoy* being scared. Remember the fairy tales; half of 'em scare the socks off you. Then the ghost stories, and the horror movies, always surefire at the box office."

He began running hot water over the dishes and I joined him at the sink, bringing the ginger ale glasses and paper napkins, my mind rushing in more directions than you could find on a map, and I grabbed hold of the first halfway logical thing that came into my head. "Well," I said, "you always know the ghost story's going to scare you and then be all over with. And when the horror movie ends you walk out into daylight."

My father was already nodding. "That ties in with one more peculiarity of the human being: We can't *really* believe we're going to die. We can be convinced of it logically, we can see proof of it, and believe that, but down in the gut where it counts, we can't. The guy next door, *he's* going to die, but not me. I'm going to enjoy the monster movie but I'm going to walk out and find the sun shining on Walnut Street, whether anybody else does or not. End of speech—but you *did* ask me."

I said, "I'm glad I did . . . I *think*."

He grinned, so I did too, and we finished cleaning up and putting things away. Then we stood there in the middle of the kitchen and I got the idea he didn't want to rush off to bed any more than I did.

Finally he said, "Well . . . Happy New Year!"

I said, "Same to you. And thanks for inviting me to your party, and—and for the speech."

Giving me a quick pat on the shoulder, he said, "Got to hand it to your mother, she sure learnt you good manners." He gave me a head start, switched off the light, and we felt our way up to bed.

I pulled the bedcovers up and wondered if I thought the end of the world was something exciting and had to admit it was. But it was scary too, and *that* was exciting. Maybe I hadn't got too old yet, after all, to believe my father knew just about everything.

I just wished he'd have time to tell me more of it.

9

A Lunch to Remember

I SLEPT A little later than usual next morning, but not much, so I was surprised when I got downstairs to find my father hadn't slept late either. He was in his robe and slippers, same as the night before, sitting in his easy chair reading the paper. He peered at me over the top of it and said, "Well, for all the carousing we did we're early risers, you and I."

I said I guessed good habits were as hard to break as bad ones. He said he wouldn't know, not having had much experience breaking bad ones. He lowered the paper to his lap, took a sip of coffee from the cup beside him, and looked at me with a self-satisfied kind of smile, as if I was a work of art he'd just carved out of oak or something. "What have you got on your agenda for this day?"

I said I didn't usually write up my agenda before breakfast, but that there was a rumor that Ed and I might go over to Waveland, show them how to play hockey.

"Making up for lost time, are you?"

I said, "Not so much that as using up all the energy I've been storing up lately eating ice cream."

He stretched his legs farther out on his footrest and dangled his arms down to show how relaxed he was. "Funny. It doesn't seem to affect *me* that way."

"Something wrong with your metabolism, maybe."

"You know," he said, "for your height and weight you sure know a lot of big words."

"Yeah," I said. "Next thing is to learn what they mean."

He went back to his paper looking pleased and I went to the kitchen and made myself a couple of slices of toast. The custom is for my mother to take it easy on New Year's Day, so meals are pretty much what everybody can scare up for himself. I had the whole breakfast table to myself, so I got the funny papers and spread them out to read there.

After that I went up to my desk and got started on my Mr. Weinstock story for Miss Wilson while the recollection was still clear in my mind.

It took most of the morning and gave me a bad case of writer's cramp which prompted me to resolve to go to summer school and learn typing. Two advantages to that: less pain and suffering for me and a lot of goodwill from teachers and anyone else who had to read my handwriting, which had improved all it was going to by the time I was in third grade. For me writing was as hard work as pulling bent nails out of boards, and according to Felice you had to write a lot more papers and stuff when you got to high school.

That resolve crashed like so many others into the same old stone wall. I wasn't going to *go* to high school. I wasn't going to learn typing or anything else.

Just about all I'd ever know, I knew already. And if I was going to read any more books and stories I'd better get started fast. That made me think of the big old city library downtown where I'd spent a lot of time ever since my father first took me there when I was eight.

Overlooking the river, with a view of the state capitol on the high ground to the east, it's built of big stone blocks blackened by time and coal smoke. It looks as strong and solid as a castle and from the outside you'd think it might be crammed with swords and battle-axes and suits of armor with dungeons down below.

But what it really had, I thought when I was eight, was the biggest assembly of books in the world, and with the card my father helped me get, I could take out as many as I could carry. With row after row of shelves from floor to ceiling crammed with books to choose from, I felt as rich as John D. Rockefeller.

Now I thought of those books and wondered how it would be with them. Would they and the building disappear in a flash just when the people did? Or would they stay on the shelves for a thousand years, mouldering in the winter damp and baking in the heat of August until they turned into smelly dust, and finally the wind and rain found their way inside and the shelves began to crumble. . . .

Leave it to me to think of the saddest, gloomiest, longest-lasting ways for things to come to an end. I was getting to be an expert.

I decided maybe I'd had too much of my own company, and anyway, I was getting hungry, so I put all that hard work in a special notebook for Miss Wilson and went down to the kitchen again and made myself a sandwich. I was just finishing when Uncle Art came in wearing a flannel robe and looking whiskery and frowsy. I looked him over and said, "Looks like the choirmaster was pretty rough on you."

Groping in the cupboard for a coffee mug he said, "Nobody ever tell you children aren't supposed to speak until spoken to?" He reached for the coffeepot at the back of the stove, burned his fingers, and swore.

I waved what was left of my sandwich toward the drainboard where I'd left the makings. "Help yourself," I said, stuffing the last bite into my mouth.

He made a sick face and said, "I'd rather die. Come to think of it, maybe I will." Then he poured himself a cup and wandered off toward the living room.

This cheered me up considerably so I phoned Ed and asked if he felt up to another session at Waveland. He said, sure he felt up to it but he couldn't because he was going with his folks to a big midday feed at the Hyperion Club, which is the golf and country club they belong to. He even sounded enthusiastic about it, saying it was a huge buffet—"Just about everything there is to eat: ham and fried chicken and roast beef and six kinds of cheese and a dozen kinds of dessert."

It sounded plenty good to me but I said, "Well, all right, if you want to load your body down with a lot of stuff it doesn't need instead of getting out on the ice and doing it some real good—"

He said, "Uh huh. And when was the last time *you* turned down a big feed?"

Always the last word.

The next day we did go, and again the day after, and before I was ready for it here came Thursday, the day school was taking up again. It seemed a dumb thing to do when they could just as well have waited until Monday, but then there are all kinds of things schools do that don't make sense to me.

I went to school in the sour and sort of hopeless mood that usually follows a vacation. All I wanted to do was live through it without dying of boredom. I should have remembered those forces of Fate and had a little faith. They weren't through with me yet.

But that's something I didn't know during second period—American History—when I got fed up to the ears with reading about the Louisiana Purchase and making notes. It seemed to me I'd been studying the Louisiana Purchase ever since I was born, so I went to work instead on an idea I'd had about a poster to put up on the school bulletin board announcing the literary competition. I'd been fooling around with the idea for several days, and this seemed a good time to put it on paper. With the history book propped up on my desk I printed a crude version of the poster on a sheet of notebook paper and thought, after a few corrections, that it turned out pretty good.

Good old Louisiana Purchase! If it hadn't bored me into doing that little job the whole day would have turned out awful instead of memorable. It started getting memorable at lunchtime when I went through the cafeteria line—spaghetti and meat sauce again —and was looking around for a place to sit when a waving arm caught my eye. The arm belonged to Judy Felton and she was looking straight at me. Or so it seemed. But I couldn't believe it, so I looked around to see if there was somebody in back of me. I saw no face with a joyful smile on it. I looked at Judy again

and she was still looking straight at me. *Me.* She
nodded and made the word *you* with her lips. Well,
you can't make an exaggerated *you* without consider-
able puckering, and the sight of Judy puckering lifted
me a foot off the floor and wafted me along like
dandelion fuzz to where she sat at the end of one of the
long tables.

She smiled, seeming to indicate she didn't see
anything really repulsive about me. But how come?
On the phone she sure hadn't made me think I was the
answer to her dreams or anything near it. Now she
patted the bench beside her. I played hard to get for
at least an eighth of a second, then I sat down.

"I just had to talk to you," she said, looking serious.
"When you didn't call again—you know, about the
Highlight competition—I was afraid I'd been rude,
cutting you off that way."

I mumbled something dumb about not having even
thought about it. She gave her head a little shake,
frowning. "I don't like to hurt people's feelings."

Just "people's"? Why not Tim Walden's? She went
on, "I was all flustered about my dress, and the party,
and—and everything, so—"

I broke in. "Gosh sake, you don't have anything to
apologize about. I just picked a lousy time to call."

"But I—"

"But nothing. I didn't think a thing about it." It
didn't really *seem* like a lie.

"Well, *I* thought about it."

"Anyway . . ." The second lie came easier than the
first. "Anyway, I decided we didn't need to make
those arrangements right away so I didn't need to
bother you with it in the first place." I took a mouth-

ful of the spaghetti to shown how relaxed I was about the whole thing. It was even colder now than when I'd got it.

"Well, that's a load off my mind," Judy said, showing just a hint of a dimple. "Speaking of the contest, have you had any brilliant ideas for publicity?"

Well, this beat finding a twenty-dollar bill! If it hadn't been for history class boredom I'd have had to mumble about this vague idea I had, but with nothing to show for it, which would have been worse than a cramp under water. Instead, I could say offhandedly, "I made a rough draft of a poster for the announcement. It's in my notebook in my locker, but if you have a sheet of paper I can make a copy from memory." I figured my memory could handle something only two hours old.

She had paper. I borrowed a pencil too and said, "It won't look right because I'm no good at printing or drawing, but . . ." I hesitated a second. Should I risk everything on one throw of the dice? Swashbuckling Tim Walden whispered, *Go for broke!* and I went on, ". . . but I'm going to get my sister to make the poster. She's really good at all that art stuff."

Naturally there was no telling whether Felice would make the poster but I could persuade her; I *had* to. I'd even *pay* her. I started in with the pencil and paper and after a minute Judy said, "You could eat at the same time, couldn't you—so it won't get cold?"

"It was cold when I got it," I said. "But it's a good idea; I usually try to avoid hunger." By concentrating hard I got a forkful into my mouth without leaving any on the outside, then got to work with the pencil. It isn't as hard for me to eat and write at the same time as it would be for most people. I write left-handed but eat with the right.

This peculiarity didn't escape Judy's notice for long and she asked me about it. I explained that I'd started off eating left-handed but my mother trained me out of it. "Insisted she couldn't have me looking like a savage at the dinner table."

This got me a ripple of laughter and she said, "You should have told her savages eat with *both* hands!"

It took a little time but I came up with an answer. "Had *you* ever heard of a savage when you were two-and-a-half years old?"

Another ripple, then, "I'll quit interrupting you so you can concentrate."

If she'd only known, she was interrupting me by just being there. I buckled down and by the time I'd eaten all I wanted of my lunch I was ready. I handed her the sheet, apologizing for the way it looked, which was nothing to the way I pictured it when Felice was through with it.

The creation I handed her looked about like this:

WANTED: AUTHORS!

Poets — Story Writers — Humorists

(Anyone but Plagiarists)

THE HIGHLIGHT

Literary Edition Needs YOU

For Spring Competition

Hemingway Was an Eighth Grader Once, So

SEND IN YOUR MASTERPIECES

REWARD IS PUBLICATION

Below that I'd printed the names of the committee
and said to submit manuscripts to any of them. In the
margins I'd penciled in a lot of squiggles to represent
whatever decorative effects Felice might want to put
in. She was sure to think of plenty. As I handed it over
to Judy I had an unexpected attack of stage fright. It
was like taking a puppy into the show ring worrying it
might throw up on the judge's shoes.

My luck held. First her eyes crinkled up, then she
smiled, gave a couple of little snorts that could have
been almost a laugh. Then she raised those greeny
eyes to mine and said, "Tim, it's *great*. It's cute and
funny. *Sure* to get their attention."

"Well," I said modestly, "it will when Felice—that's
my sister—gets through with it." Having a little
modesty left over, I added, "You should suggest any
changes you might think would improve it—you and
the others when they see it."

She shook her head. "I wouldn't change a word—
and I'll say so if I'm asked."

The ugly sound of the buzzer signaling end of lunch
hour lowered my altitude considerably and we both
stood up automatically and picked up our trays.

I scrambled through my already scrambled brain for
a windup line. Uncle Art would have thought of half a
dozen. About a second before it would have been too
late I got one. "Well, thanks for lunch. I'll leave the
tip."

"Spendthrift!"

I spent the rest of the school day not learning things
while I devoted the time to trying to decide if I was
getting anywhere with Judy after all, or just treading
water. She'd invited me to sit with her all right, but

not because she craved my company. Just to apologize. What I couldn't get over was the subject of the apology. The message I'd got over the phone was definitely cloudy and cool. On the other hand, it had been sunny and warm at lunch.

I bounced around all afternoon between hope and discouragement and ended up with the conclusion that I'd gained a few yards but somebody kept moving the goalpost. No quitting, though. Just hang onto the ball and keep charging, I told myself sturdily.

After dinner that night I craftily began laying the groundwork for getting Felice to do my poster. The dishes were all piled up and we were about to start when I said, as if the idea was born that minute, "Tell you what! I'm not doing anything special tonight, so why don't I just do the whole thing?"

She gave me a prosecuting-attorney look. "What's the catch? What do you want from me?"

"Well, *gee!*" I said, deeply hurt. "Can't a guy do somebody a favor just because he *wants* to?"

"Not if his name's Timothy Walden."

I told her that was a cruel thing to say but I'd overlook it.

"*Saint* Timothy."

"Well, all right," I said sadly. "If that's the way you feel about it, I won't—"

Right there I saw a change in her expression—something about her eyes that meant she'd thought of something she'd a lot rather do right now than wash dishes—and she said, "Oh no you don't!"

"Don't what?"

"Weasel out. Was that a bonafide offer or wasn't it?"

"Durn tootin' it was, but—"

"No buts about it. If it was a genuine offer, no strings attached, I accept!"

"No strings," I said. It wasn't exactly a lie, just a sort of rearrangement of the truth.

Felice vanished from the kitchen with the speed of sound, leaving me with my victory. I hoped it would be worth it because the cost was sky-high. Nobody in his right mind has ever *enjoyed* doing dishes.

By the time I'd slaved my way through them all and put them away I was beginning to feel as if I really had done it out of the kindness of my heart and was thinking pretty highly of myself when the phone rang. It was Ed.

"Snow looks about right. What do you say?"

"You mean tonight?"

He took time to think. "Guess not. It's after eight."

"That's right," I said. "Our folks would get suspicious if we said we were going sliding this late."

"Tomorrow evening, then. About seven, okay?"

"Uh, sure," I said. "Only . . ."

"Only what?"

"Nothing," I said. "We'd better skip it." The *only* was because a swarm of butterflies had taken to the air in my stomach. This talk of "tomorrow" had done it. Tomorrow was Saturday, and Saturday would be my first boxing lesson. Tomorrow evening at seven I might be too beat up to even *carry* a sled.

CHAPTER

10

The Manly Art

IN THE MORNING the butterflies woke up at the same time I did. They were still on the job that afternoon when I checked out the wire basket containing my gym clothes and went to the locker room and got into my trunks and Keds while pretending I wasn't sizing up the bunch of other guys who were doing the same thing. In the gym Red Clifford was waiting with a roster sheet. He checked us in, then issued boxing gloves and introduced the instructor, who was a young guy who fought in local matches under the name Kid McClusky, in the lightweight class. He was wearing a sweatsuit with his name on the back in big green letters.

The "ring" was several tumbling mats dragged together in a corner of the gym. He paired the nine of us off, two and two, and took the odd guy as his opponent. Then he stood off to one side and made a speech. You could tell he'd made the same speech before.

"Boxin' is a sport," he began. "It ain't a form of

combat, like them old gladiators. We wanna outpoint the other fella, not kill 'im. Wanna kill 'im we'll grab a club, or a gun, not a pair of boxin' gloves." He paused for the laugh, and we obliged, once we'd caught on. "So what we're gonna do here is learn the bazic skills so we'll know how to handle ourself an' have a little fun too.

"Okay." (Actually he said "'Kay.") "'Kay. First of all me an' my sparrin' pardner here are gonna demonstrate the bazic moves: jab, block, punch, block, counterpunch. Then we'll all do it." He swung around facing his partner and went into the boxer's crouch, left hand leading, right cocked close to his chin. The pupil did the same and Kid McClusky said, "Gonna jab at his face. Hurt him some if I can, but mainly it's to keep him off balance, keep him away from me, set 'im up for a right-hand punch. Now he can duck, dodge, or block the jab, but he better stay on his toes for the right he knows is comin' his way."

He went through the motions, visibly pulling his punches, any one of which could have made the guy wish he'd stayed home. When he'd run through the drill he barked out, "'Kay! Ever'body square off now an' we'll run through it!"

My partner was Tod somebody; I'd seen him around, played pool or billiards with him. We looked at each other and he halfway grinned. "Okay, Tiger," he said, "let's get at it." So we did, throwing punches and blocking them about as well as you'd expect of a couple of greenhorns. After a minute Kid McClusky yelled, "Hold it!" Everybody stood still and he said, looking right at me, "You there, come over here." He sent the kid he'd been demonstrating with over to take my place and said to me, "Okay—pretend you'n me'r about to get into a scrap. You're gonna knock my block off. Show me how you're gonna start out."

Well, he was the boss, so I remembered what he'd said about going into a crouch, chin tucked behind my shoulder, stuck my right hand out and held the left back.

He said, "Thought so! Class—we got us a little problem. This here's a southpaw. Whatever I tell you to do with the right hand, he's gonna wanna do with the left, and it'll throw you off. Well, maybe that ain't a bad thing. In the ring you gotta be ready for anything. For right now, while we're learnin' the bazics, I'll keep this kid—what's yer name?" I told him. "I'll keep Tim here for my sparring pardner an' I'll shift to the lefty stance so's he won't be confused and neither will you fellas."

He paused and sort of smirked, so I knew a wise-crack was on the way. "I'll have to keep the ol' brain workin' or he's li'ble to clean my clock." Everybody laughed, me included. "Okay—we'll run through it again now. And remember—keep movin'! Don't just stand like a cigar-store Inyun. Movin' target's harder to hit."

Shuffling around obediently, we jabbed, blocked, countered, threw left hooks, right crosses, and upper-cuts on command. Pretty soon Kid McClusky said, "C'mon, Tim—put a little *steam* in them punches. Lemme see what you got in that left hand!" He stuck out his chin. "Hit it—it ain't gonna break!"

I told myself I had about as much chance hitting that chin as I would Jack Dempsey's, but I took aim and let fly with everything I had. He could have blocked it easy, but he didn't and it landed with a jolt I felt all the way to my shoulder. It felt *good*, and I remembered to cover up the way he'd told us to, ready to block a counterpunch with both hands and elbows. Naturally he could have uncorked one and knocked me halfway across the gym, but instead he grinned and said, "Nice goin', kid. I *felt* that. You got somethin' in that left all right. But instead of coverin' you shoulda follad it with a right to my belly—set me up for an uppercut with the ol' left. But nemmine, we ain't that far along yet. Okay, fellas—if you was watchin' you saw me take a punch—and it was a good one. But we ain't here to hurt each other, we're here to learn. Le's go back now an' run through the drill again. Put yer guard up, ever'body!"

For the rest of the hour, and while we were showering and getting dressed, I kept telling myself to quit feeling this sort of glow inside, as if I'd really *done* something. What had happened? I'd been singled out for special attention because I was left-handed, which was an act of God and no credit to me. And I'd landed a punch on the chin of a professional fighter, which I couldn't have done in a year if he hadn't let me. But it wasn't either of those things really; it was what that punch had done to *me*. I could still feel it, and it still made me think, "Hey, maybe this is something I can do—or anyway learn to do—maybe even get good at." Maybe after all I wasn't the marshmallow I'd always suspected I was.

After dinner that night I went down to the basement and about wore myself out shadowboxing—dancing around throwing punches, blocking, counterpunching, all of it. This wasn't as dumb as it sounds. Kid

McClusky had recommended going through the motions, only he said it was best if you had a big mirror so you could watch yourself and maybe spot some things you were doing wrong. He'd also said it would be good to work on the punching bags in the exercise room in between lessons. I figured that wouldn't do for me, not wanting to tip my hand to Dunk Bolander, and I got to wondering if I could rig up a punching bag down in the basement. Trouble was I didn't have any idea what it would cost to buy one. I had four dollars or so left from my snow shoveling, which couldn't be anywhere near enough.

Hit by a faint hope, I hunted up the morning paper and went through the want ads, just in case somebody wanted to sell a punching bag dirt cheap. No luck. There weren't any for sale at any price.

As I was refolding the paper my eye was caught by a headline across the top of an inside page: WORLD'S END WORRIES MOUNT SWIFTLY ACROSS NATION. Beneath were a lot of photographs. One showed an open-air amphitheater jammed with people praying and palm trees all around. The caption said that those people were in Florida somewhere "seeking solace through prayer."

Another picture showed a delegation of inmates of a prison somewhere appealing to the warden to set them free to spend their final hours at home. Another showed an Army officer speaking to an auditorium full of soldiers. The caption told about armed forces chaplains being deluged with requests for home leave during the last days of April so the men could be with their families.

There were more pictures and the gist of the story

was that Americans from all sections of the country and all walks of life were "deeply concerned" about the predicted May Day calamity. Their numbers, it went on, were between thousands and hundreds of thousands. Whatever the number, it told me I sure had a lot of company. And *that* made me think of my father's New Year's party speech. How many of those people, I wondered, had read about old Mergenbreit and the apocalyptic writings and been convinced that way, and how many had just got caught up in the fearful excitement, the way my father said?

Well, brooding about it wasn't going to get me any answers. Right here and now my problem was the punching bag, and I didn't know how to proceed on that. I still didn't know after dinner when I was trying to concentrate on a book. I was making pretty slow going of it when something caught my attention. A smell. Cigar smoke. It didn't smell quite as bad as my father's cigars, so it must be Uncle Art's. Why hadn't I thought of him until now? I headed downstairs.

In the game room I cleared my throat so he'd know I was coming, and eased in through the furnace room doorway. Uncle Art was sitting in my father's beat-up old easy chair, smoke curling around his head, legs stretched out in front of him. He was reading a magazine called *Modern Merchandising*. I said, "If you don't want me to interrupt you, I won't."

He said, "You already did, but mentioning it was a graceful touch. What can I do for you?"

"Just wondering," I said, "if you'd know how to go about finding a second-hand punching bag for sale cheap."

He put the magazine down on his lap. "The things

you ask," he said, then blew some more smoke and watched it rise up, and added thoughtfully, "Punching bag. Now that's an item we don't have much call for at National Cigar. I take it you're asking me to canvass my wide circle of acquaintances and come up with the identity of a man who deals in used sporting goods."

"There's always a chance," I said.

He thought some more, finally said, "Nothing leaps to mind. You try the want ads?"

I told him I had, which called for more thinking, then he said, "I'll ask around."

I said the next day would be soon enough and he came back with, "Nice to know you're not in a big hurry." He peered at the hot end of his cigar as if he was consulting it about something. Then he said, "Don't mean to be nosy, sport, but I'm just the *teensiest* bit curious. Not going after the Golden Gloves, are you?"

I was halfway ready for this. After all, it was only natural he'd be curious, me having never shown any interest in such a thing before. I'd thought of saying I needed more exercise, wanted to stay in shape, that sort of thing. But I knew he'd get the truth out of me in the end, so I told him the whole story of Dunk Bolander, without mentioning the other things on my list. In the middle of it he shoved the footstool that had begun life as an oyster box toward me.

So I told the rest of the story sitting down and by the time I'd finished, the cigar had gone out owing to lack of attention. He fired it up again and waved the match around to put it out, peering at me through the swirling smoke. "Well, Tim," he said at last, "it looks to me like you've got your head screwed on right. If you've got to fight it makes a lot of sense to be as ready as you can get. If you're ready, and the other fella knows it, chances are you won't have to fight him after all."

"Did you used to get in fights?" I wanted to know.

"A few," said Uncle Art. "When I couldn't talk my way out of it."

"Did you win?"

He had to think that over, then said, "Hard to tell sometimes. But I always *claimed* I did. Got so I believed it, which was just as good."

I said I wished I could believe it in advance. "I could use a little confidence. But the fact is I could get my block knocked off."

"You could," he said, nodding slowly, "but I've got a hunch you won't."

I said, "Well, don't bet any money on it."

After a little bit he said, "Tell you what. I'll make a bet *this* way: If I can make a deal on a punching bag I'll buy it for you. If you lose your fight you won't have to pay me back. Now, if that isn't confidence, show me what is."

"It's a deal," I said. "But I wish the odds were more in your favor."

"Not betting on the odds," said Uncle Art. "Betting on my sister's boy. Kid with gumption."

I stared at him. If I had gumption, this was the first time I'd heard about it. But I could see he was serious. "Well, thanks," I said. Didn't seem quite enough, so I added, "Sure hope I have to pay you back."

I went back upstairs and read until I got sleepy. While I was undressing I looked out the window. It was snowing again.

CHAPTER
11

A Little Man-Talk

THE WEEK AFTER New Year's, the weather worried itself into another state of indecision. It stayed cold but it would cloud up and get set to snow, then after a few useless flurries lose its nerve and clear off for a few hours before starting in to do the whole thing over again.

By Tuesday afternoon there was a four- or five-inch cover of fluffy new snow, enough to spoil any chance of hitching rides but not enough to do any good. I spent most of the afternoon over at Ed's playing checkers and peering gloomily out the windows. Finally the sky lightened up, looking as if it might stay that way for a while, and I decided to give the Weinstocks' walks one more sweeping. I wanted to erase Felice's drawing, which probably looked a little shabby by this time, and maybe the Weinstocks had seen enough of it anyway.

Grabbing the broom from the garage, I headed on over, hearing what sounded like hammering as I passed the side door. Maybe my father had come home early and was starting to build the shelves he'd been talking about. I didn't stop to find out.

With the broom I stirred up a minor blizzard all the way around Weinstock's house and was ending up at the back porch when Mr. Weinstock came out wearing his smoking jacket but not smoking. When he got out his little coin purse again I said there was no charge for sweeping when I'd already got paid for shoveling, but he said, "For a couple inches maybe, but for this much I pay." He gave me a quarter, which I tried to refuse, but he stuck it into the palm of my mitten and closed my fist around it. "No arguments, please." So I thanked him and told him I'd erased the drawing, and why. He thought about it a minute and finally nodded. "I'll miss it," he said. "It was a . . . a joy to me. But your reasoning is correct." I didn't know what to say to that, but he wasn't finished anyway. "No, not reasoning, instinct. Your instinct is to do the proper thing. I have noticed it before."

I mumbled, which is what I do best at a time like that, and made departure noises. He just smiled, patted my shoulder, and said, "Good-bye, Timmie."

I headed for home, thinking, Wow, with all those great instincts maybe I ought to go into a more restful kind of business.

Sitting on the stair-landing steps to take off my galoshes, I heard voices below and caught the reek of cigar smoke again. Maybe a little man-talk might be restful. I could tell them all about my instincts.

The furnace room was as smoky as a barbecue pit. They both looked up as I came in and Uncle Art said, "Well, hey—reinforcements! Have a cigar?"

"Some other time," I said.

"Just as well," my father said. "There's barely enough air down here for the two of us."

"We take turns breathing," Uncle Art said, looking at the hot end of his cigar. Then he cleared his throat. "Your dad and I," he went on, "have been addressing the subject of punching bags."

I pricked up my ears at that. "Did you find one?"

He tilted his head. "Take a look in there."

"In there" was the room beyond the furnace room. It's still called the coal room even though we haven't burned coal for a long time.

I looked, switching on the overhead light. There it was, a punching bag hanging from the ceiling in the far corner right underneath the back porch. I stepped closer. It was suspended from the center of a four-foot square of new lumber bolted to the joists—a surface from which the bag would rebound. It had to have been built by my father, with Uncle Art as helper. They must have been working most of the time I'd been out of the house.

I stepped up, gave it a couple of quick lefts and rights, and went back to the door, saying, "Wow! It's keen—really keen! Thanks!"

"You can't even imagine the trouble we went to," Uncle Art said.

"You get a bargain?" I said.

"Any cheaper it would have been theft."

My father said, "If you look close you'll see we mounted the overhead on squares of inner-tube rubber. Cut down the noise a little in case your mother might find it, ah, irksome." A little pause and he went on, "Which brings up a question: Have you told her what you're up to?"

I admitted I hadn't, and he said, "Didn't think so. Well, when you go to whaling away at that thing she can't possibly help hearing it. You ready to tell her the whole truth and nothing but?"

Uncle Art answered for me. "Not the *whole* truth, Frank! It would be too painful for her. Manly art of self-defense—every boy should learn it—YMCA recommends it—that's the pitch to give her! Strong minds in strong bodies—self-reliance—fearless in the face of—"

"Art!" my father said forcefully. "You're using too much air! Besides, you can't expect Tim to say all that to his mother."

Uncle Art looked thoughtful, but in no time at all he rose to the occasion. "All right, I'll give her the message myself. Eloquence is a powerful weapon!"

My father said, "Every family should have a good con man. Just don't overdo it."

"Do I ever? Tim, you're in good hands!"

They both looked at me, sort of pleased, so I had the floor and didn't know what to do with it. Plain to see that my uncle had explained the whole thing to my father, so now he too knew about Dunk Bolander and my ambitions along that line—and he had pitched in and helped. They were behind me, solid as rocks, which was what made it so impossible to thank them. Uncle Art came to my rescue. "Mind if I use the bag now and then? I ever feel like poking someone in the eye, I'll come and poke that instead. Safer."

My father got into the act too. "Not me. I might wreck it. Never did know my own strength."

Between them they uncorked me and I managed to say, "If I ever figure out how to do it right, I'll thank you. It's . . . it's *terrific*."

They didn't seem to expect any more in the way of gratitude, so I went up to the living room where my mother was reading *Collier's* magazine. She looked up, then wrinkled her nose. "Phew! You smell like a dead cigar!"

"Sorry," I said. "I've been hanging around with some low company."

She sniffed. "Well, that's not hard to find in this house!"

"Figured I might raise the moral level a little down there."

"Well, best of luck," she said, smiling a little.

I don't know when Uncle Art tackled my mother about the punching bag and boxing lessons, but I knew he'd done it because I worked out several times on the bag, making the kind of racket you'd expect, and she never said anything about it, although she looked at me sort of tight-lipped once or twice.

She did say something, though, when Saturday rolled around again and I was about to leave for the Y. All she said was, "If you *must* do it I suppose you must. But do be careful. Don't take chances."

"Don't worry," I said. "Not taking chances is what I specialize in."

At the lesson I took no chances but still didn't do a great job of taking care of myself. Kid McClusky drilled us this time on blocking and counterpunching, and I can testify it's a thousand times easier to block a punching bag than a punch. He appointed himself my sparring partner again, and it didn't do much for my self-confidence to find out how easy it was for him to hit me. He'd jab fast with his right, which wasn't even natural to him, and either break through my guard or evade it altogether and I'd get a glove in my face. He was pulling his punches of course and wore the same fat training gloves we all did. It didn't hurt me but I could feel the jar of it every time. Then I'd throw a left at him and he'd either block it or sway backwards so I'd miss altogether or hit him a lick that might have been real upsetting to a baby.

Now and then he'd fire a command at me. "Get that shoulder up! Tuck your chin behind it!" Or "Bring your left forward! Ain't doing you no good way back there like throwin' rocks!"

The other guys got yelled at too. "You guys all got flat feet? Move! Up on your toes—keep movin'!" It wasn't encouraging to know he could block my punches, whack me in the face, and watch the other guys at the same time.

When he called a break he faced me sort of earnestly. "Loosen up, kid," he said. "You're tight as a git-tar string. Here—like this." He waggled his shoulders, letting his arms hang loose at his sides. They flapped around like a skeleton in the wind. He raised his voice. "Okay, ever'body do that." We all did. There were a few grins. It looked pretty funny.

Kid McCluskey spoke louder still. "That's the ticket! Laugh's good for loosenin' up with."

This set off a lot of loud, forced laughing and clowning around. Guys were waggling like crazy and laughing like idiots and falling down to show how loosened up they were. For a while he let them carry on, then let go with a bellow. "QUIET!" Everybody settled down and he said, "Tell ya what we're gonna do now. We're gonna do a drill by the numbers. We ain't gonna hit each other, we're just gonna go through the motions. 'Kay. Each pair decide who's number one. I'll call one, two, one, two. On *one* Number One will punch and Number Two will block; on *two*, do it backwards, Number Two counterpunching and Number One blocking. Got it?"

Everybody nodded and he went on, "It's an exercise, see? Help you make these moves automatic'ly, so's you don't hafta think about it." To me he said, "You're Number One;" then, guard up, he crouched down to nearer my level. "Okay, fellas—one-two, one-two, one-two . . ." We all punched, blocked, and counterpunched until I, for one, was sucking air like a played-out mountain climber.

Finally he yelled, "Hold it—that's all for now!" Everybody let their arms fall to their sides and stood around gasping and sweating.

He gave us about five minutes to get our breath, then put us to work, four at a time, on the two heavy punching bags that hung near the back wall.

He kept us at it until we were about to drop, then sent us, four by four, to the showers.

When I got home the first person I ran into was Felice, who was at the kitchen sink washing out some garment or other. "Well thank goodness," she said. "I'm glad you got here before sometime next week!"

I said, "If I'm late for something, it's news to me. What is it?"

She wrung out whatever it was and dried her hands. "Mother said you'd help me move my furniture."

"Didn't tell *me* about it. Move it where?"

"*Around*, of course, not *out*." She was irritated because I didn't know something I couldn't have known.

I guess *I* started looking irritated too, because she suddenly decided to change her tune. "I'd really appreciate it, Timmie. I just want to put my desk where my bed is, and vice versa, and, oh, a couple of other things."

I was about to say "a couple" would turn out to be twenty when I suddenly thought of my poster and did a quick shift. "Sure thing, Felice. I'll just change into my furniture-mover outfit and be right with you."

I pitched in and did everything she told me to, including moving the desk three times after we'd already moved it across the room—two inches this way, two inches that way, then one inch back. It didn't take much more than half an hour to put everything just where she wanted it.

When she was satisfied she flopped down in her desk chair and looked all around appreciatively. "Now *that's* more like it! Don't you think so?"

"Durn betcha," I said, lying helpfully, although I couldn't really see a lot of improvement. She seemed to expect more out of me, so I gambled an observation. "It's more, uh, balanced."

My luck was in. She looked pleased. "That's it! That's *exactly* what it is!"

I thought, Well, there'll never be a better chance, so I took the plunge. "I've been thinking of asking you to do *me* a favor."

She didn't look quite so pleased. "What kind of favor?"

"Could you make a poster for me?"

She thought a minute, frowning a little. "Well, I might. What *kind* of poster?"

"Mostly words," I said. "I've got a kind of model printed out in my notebook."

She sighed. "Go get it."

I brought it and she read it over and didn't say anything, which I took for a vote of no confidence until I saw she was looking at it with squinted eyes, doing artist stuff in her head. After a while she said, "I'll do a preliminary sketch on regular drawing paper, then do it on illustration board. You'll have to get a sheet of it for me, down at Younkers' art supply department. Good quality. Probably cost you about fifty-five cents."

Fifty-five cents. Hour or so's work with a snow shovel, I thought. Oh well—easy come, easy go. I said, "Okay—and thanks for taking on the job. I sure appreciate it."

"When do you have to have it?"

I wasn't sure, but I said, "Week or so?"

"Easy. If I work it right my teacher'll let me use class time."

Suddenly remembering, I said, "Gee, I didn't tell you—all those squiggles I put around the edges are for illustrations. Anything you can think of."

"I'm way ahead of you," she said loftily. "Got a few ideas already."

I should have known. And I could put up with a lot more loftiness than that; my poster was already taking shape inside Felice's head. I couldn't believe it would be anything but a big success, and all for the price of a little furniture moving. And fifty-five cents.

CHAPTER

12

A Very Close Shave

ON SUNDAY THE weather settled down. Still cold, some sunshine, but no new snow. Ed and I walked part of the proposed hitching route—as far as Ingersoll—and decided the time had come. Monday, right after dinner. It looked to be a great day—but the best part was one I had no way of knowing about.

After the last bell rang I was heading down the hall toward my locker—me and a couple hundred other people—when I heard a voice I'd have recognized in the middle of a riot. "Timmie! Timmie, *wait!*"

I stopped so suddenly two people caromed off me like billiard balls. I turned around. "Oh!" I said, real surprised. "Hi, Judy."

She looked like the newest penny in the piggy bank and she said, "Timmie, have you got a second?"

"Take an hour," I said. It just popped out. Wow—maybe I was learning!

She laughed, but just then somebody banged into her and she put her hand on my arm and pushed. "Let's get out of the middle."

We made it into a classroom doorway where there

was barely room for both of us and she said, "Just wanted to ask you . . ."

She didn't take her hand off my arm right away and it was sending electrical charges into me.

I looked into her eyes, which sort of blurred, and all of a sudden I went into a couple seconds' worth of total insanity. The thundering herd in the hall suddenly went silent and something babbled at me, *What if you'd just grab her right now, and kiss her, and . . .* At that instant she dropped her hand and sanity returned, bringing me a case of trembly knees.

". . . how you're getting along with that nifty poster," she finished.

"My sister's working on it now," I said, sounding almost normal. "She's got some great ideas."

"Wonderful! When do you think she'll be finished?"

"End of the week," I said recklessly, and added even more recklessly, "As soon as it's finished I'll bring it to school and show you."

She smiled just enough to dimple up a little and said, "You mean me and the rest of the committee?"

"Well, uh, sure." I'd forgotten there *was* a committee. Uncle Art would have said that to her, but my nerve wasn't up to it.

Judy shifted the books she was carrying to a more comfortable position. "Well, that's good news, Timmie. I can hardly wait to see it."

Then she was gone, leaving me to work out whether I'd been heading up the hall or down it, and what I'd planned to do when I got to the end of it. Fortunately I recovered in time to sprint for the streetcar that had stopped out at the corner. Made it just as its bell clanged to signal it was about to move. I had to go down to Younker Brothers to get the illustration board for the poster.

It cost me sixty-five cents instead of fifty-five, but that wasn't the worst of it. The size was what staggered me, and the fact that it couldn't be rolled up, the way I'd expected. Felice had ordered a sheet forty by thirty-two inches. I'd expected it to be a thick sheet of paper that could be made into a big roll for carrying. But this was like a heavy cardboard only with one side white and smooth.

When I asked the salesgirl, who was about eighteen, if she could roll it just enough so that one end would be just barely over the other, she looked at me like I was four years old and feeble-minded and said, "I could if you wanted it broken in two." She proceeded to wrap it in about four yards of brown paper and made a little handle at one end with a loop of twine that didn't look too strong.

Getting home with that thing was about the hardest work I ever did. I could carry it with both hands providing I didn't want to see where I was going, or I could clamp one arm over it and hold the corner with my other hand.

The clamp worked pretty well until I made it outside, where the wind turned my unwieldy package into a sail that tried to send me smashing into the side of a building or into the middle of the street. It wasn't really much of a wind, just a fair breeze that couldn't make up its mind where it was going. I had to shift quick to the two-hand method in order to hang onto the monster. The breeze would catch the forward end from first one side then the other, or else hit it head-on and try to wrap it around my body. I staggered and lurched from side to side or came almost to a stop then plunged forward, barely missing lamp-posts, mailboxes, and people only with the aid of superhuman strength. That package was alive, crafty, and full of ill will. Much as it resented me I resented it more, and downright loathed the people who grinned at the sight of my drunken performance.

Against all probability I made it onto the streetcar, off it again, and the rest of the way home. Felice took the poster board from me, unwrapped it, examined it carefully, and said, "Well, you *did* manage to get it here in one piece." Then she handed me all that wrapping paper and said, "Do something with this, will you?"

After an ordeal like that I didn't see how I could get up the energy to go out hitching rides, but after loading up on second helpings of everything at dinner I was ready for anything. I was out at the end of the drive with my sled when Ed came whistling his way around the corner. He was wearing a wool stocking cap. On my head, as usual, was my father's worn old fur hat with a bill and ear-flaps you could turn down.

Ed said, "We really doing this? I thought it'd never happen."

We fell into step, heading south, carrying our sleds across our backs as always.

"We're doing it, all right," I said. "What'll you bet we make it?"

"Won't bet. Betting's bad luck."

"You still got the route in mind?" I said. "Been a long time since I told you."

He recited it. "Here to Ingersoll, Ingersoll to Polk, Polk to University, University to Thirty-fifth, and back here. One hour to do it in, counting from the first ride we get. And if we have to walk more than one block the deal's off and we start over next time."

It sounded easy but I knew it wasn't. The total distance was under three miles and if everything went perfectly we could do it in half the allowed time. But nothing ever went perfectly as we both knew from experience. I'd made it hard to do, so we'd know we'd really done something and it would be worth a place on my list.

"One thing you forgot," I said. "If one of us misses a ride the one that gets it has to let go and come back to that point."

"I didn't forget it, we just don't need it. It's what we do all the time anyway."

By now we'd crossed to the west side of Thirty-fifth and were ready to begin the slow slide down to Rollins. It was a good spot because on that corner was Borrusch's Drugstore with the Piggly Wiggly right next to it, so people came and went pretty steadily. It's pretty bright, with a streetlight on the corner and more lights from the store windows, so you have to be careful. Some drivers don't care if you hitch on but some will jump out and chase you away if they see you, so you do your best not to be seen.

Pretty soon a man came out of the Piggly Wiggly with a sack of groceries which he put in on the passenger's side, then went around and got into the driver's seat. Ed and I looked at each other but made no move except to tense up. There was plenty of room ahead of the man's car. He wouldn't have to back up, so we'd have to move fast. The starter tried once and failed, then the engine caught. Needing no conversation about it, we scooped up our sleds and moved up behind the car in a crouch and put the sleds down and flopped onto them.

Almost instantly we moved out and around the parked car ahead and were on our way. Or so we thought. To my disgust the car turned east at the next corner. Wrong way altogether. We let go, digging our toes into the snow to stop. Back to the corner for another try. No use moaning about it. Happened all the time.

Ed said, "Hope it isn't going to be like this the whole trip. We'll be all night."

"Can't be," I said. "Never has before."

When we got back to the corner another car had replaced the first one. It was a big new Pierce-Arrow sedan. Maroon—really spiffy. Ed said, "Well, hey! Let's wait for that guy and go first class."

"They're all the same," I said, "when you're back there with the exhaust in your face."

Ahead of the fancy car was a Hudson Super-Six, behind it one of the new Ford Model-A roadsters. Sporty. The kind Uncle Art had his eye on.

First driver out got into the Hudson and we lost no time getting into position. In a few seconds we were off. The car had chains on, so we were braced for a barrage of snow chunks. When a car is accelerating those chains give you a spray like a sand-blasting hose, but it slacks off when you get up to speed. Until it does there's nothing you can do but keep your head down and squint your eyes almost shut. It was like that now until we'd passed the intersection at Center Street and got part way along toward Pleasant and it started being fun instead of punishment.

I don't know any sensation like it. Like flying, maybe, only you're in touch with the ground. Like riding on the wind. Like going off the high diving board, except that it lasts lots longer. And you're not just going along, like an amusement park ride, you're *doing* something. You're using your arms and your eyes and your ears, but most of all you're using your head, operating with the throttle all the way out. You're doing your best to keep track of what's ahead, what's behind, staying in control because if you goof there's going to be trouble.

We zipped past Pleasant Street, then Woodland, then the long block to Ingersoll where our driver would either turn or go on across the car tracks and up the hill to Grand Avenue. A right turn was what we wanted. We didn't get it. About fifty yards short of Ingersoll there's a pretty good incline, so the chains bit deeper and peppered us again, but it didn't last long because there's a stop sign at the intersection. I could tell by the way the driver kept to the center of the street instead of edging over to the right that he was either going straight on or to the left. I took a look behind and so did Ed. Car lights, but not near. We let go and scrambled over to the sidewalk by Reppert's Pharmacy. Kaufman's Grocery was next door, and a cleaning place next to that. Plenty of cars around, all facing west because Ingersoll is divided in two by the streetcar line so the eastbound traffic was all on the other side.

Being right there, we leaned our sleds next to the door and went in Reppert's and bought a candy bar each. We sat on our sleds out by the curb and ate them.

For a while nobody came out from either store, then two people did, one right after the other. One was a woman. Ed said, "Woman driver!" the way his father always does, which I took to mean he'd rather go with the man, so we kept our eyes on him. He went over to a big Packard—not new but not so old either—and we got set to move. When the driver opened the door on the other side he was turned sideways to us and I got a quick look at him before he got in. I said, "Oh, nuts! It's a high school guy." I wished we'd gone with the woman. Ed hadn't seen the guy's face because he was busy tugging his cap down in front as far as he could to shelter his eyes. He said, "Well, they aren't *all* crazy drivers."

The woman's car was already pulling away from the curb, so we had no choice unless we wanted to wait some more. "Okay," I said, and we did our crouching run to the rear of the Packard and grabbed on just in time to get a cloud of black smoke in our faces as the guy raced the engine for no reason except that he liked the noise.

He pulled out and accelerated fast. Luckily no chains, so we didn't get a real bombardment. We had got about halfway to Polk Boulevard and I'd have bet we'd make it when he suddenly swung to the right off Ingersoll. He skidded a little as he made the turn. It caught us by surprise and we had our hands full controlling the sleds with our steering levers. No chance of giving each other a signal about what to do next, so we held on. In a few seconds I realized he'd turned onto Park Lane which is really a sort of interruption to Forty-second Street with some high-class residential areas around. If he went straight on, it would turn into Forty-second again and pass the high school on the east. But he didn't. Instead, almost as soon as he turned right he turned left up a short street I didn't know. As he made the turn he skidded again, corrected, and kept going. I thought, *Uh oh, he saw us. He knows we're back here!*

The streets in this area curved around a lot, and I thought that unless he lived around here he was coming this way just to throw a scare into us, and maybe when he'd had his fun he'd head back up Forty-second. My mind was working fast, but not too efficiently, as it turned out. All I could think of was that if we bailed out now we'd have to walk more than one block, whatever direction we went, and that would cancel the project and we'd have to try it another time. No, by golly, I thought. I'm going to stick with him till I see a place to get another ride! I glanced over at Ed. What I could see of his face looked tight-jawed and determined.

From the corner of my eye I saw deep lawns and big houses swinging by as if they were on hinges and before I was really braced for it, the guy turned left, left again, skidding each time and correcting. He must be intending to circle the block, which was a small one. Left again, wheels sliding. This time he didn't make it. The big car went into a spin, and from then on it was like the awfulest nightmare I ever had in my life.

As he went into the spin I glimpsed Ed shooting off to the right. My mind made lightning calculations all on its own, about speed, angles, and distances. It told me to hang on until the car had made half a turn. My sled, acting as if it was alive, fought against my frantic efforts to slide straight instead of digging the side of a runner in. A second later I let go and the whiplash momentum of the spinning car flung me away and slightly ahead of it. I was in the middle of an area where the street widened to accommodate other streets curving in from left and right. Ahead was a curb, looking from my altitude as high as a wall. I dug my toes in and worked the steering lever like crazy to aim for a break in the curb where there was a driveway.

I didn't make it. The sled hit the curb with a teeth-rattling jar that shook me up considerably but didn't do any real harm. It took a few moments to sort out what had happened, then I looked back and instantly froze. The Packard—it was *following* me! The spin had stopped and it was sliding sideways, rear wheels a little in advance of the front ones. It moved in a slow, stately kind of way, like a building on the move. I didn't see how it could miss me.

I might have had time to scramble out of the way. I'll never know because time just stopped. I lay there, still flat on my sled except for my backward-turned head. Lay there helpless as a fried egg on a platter.

At a time like that your life is supposed to pass before you while you repent of the bad things you've done. Mine didn't. If I thought at all, which I'm not sure I did, I was just wondering in a dumb way how I could have got myself into a mess like this. But even when I couldn't see any other possible outcome I don't think I really believed the thing was going to hit me. Not *me*.

Well, obviously it didn't because here I am writing this. The Packard's right front wheel struck the curb first, the rear one a second later, about a foot or two to my left, making a nasty double-thunk sound. Immediately it leaned sharply to the right, the direction it had been going, and I thought it might topple over, but it tilted back instead and sort of teetered until it came to rest.

Now I could move. I stood up and wanted to sit down right away because my legs felt weak and trembly. Then I heard the door open on the other side and the driver came peering around the back of the car at me. He looked about sixteen and his face was the color of dirty snow. He must have thought for sure he'd find a corpse. We looked at each other, neither of us getting any pleasure out of it. Then he said one thing only: "Ye gods!", got back in the car, made gear-clashing noises, and drove away slowly and carefully.

Now here came Ed from somewhere up the street, sled under one arm, hurrying. He saw I was all in one piece and said, "Judas Priest! I thought you were a goner!"

I said, "Me too."

He peered toward where the car had just disappeared around a corner. "The rat! He was *trying* to throw us off."

"He was at first," I said. "Then he lost control and panicked. I think the brakes locked on him."

He lowered his sled to his runner points and used the steering lever to rest his arms on. "Well, what do we do now?"

I sighed. "Walk back to Ingersoll, I guess. Give up for this time."

While we walked we relived the wild ride and

agreed our big mistake was in not bailing out when the guy first turned off Ingersoll. I asked him if he'd been scared.

"Pea-green. Don't tell me you weren't!"

I thought about it and said, "Not until I saw that car sliding straight at me. Before that I was too *busy*."

Ed said, "I'm *never* too busy to be scared."

We were lucky going home. A man came out of an apartment building on Ingersoll and took us straight down the street. We got off at Thirty-fifth and after one failure got a hitch that took us all the way home. When I went in I was surprised to see by the kitchen clock it was only nine. All of that had happened in only an hour and a half. In the living room my father was reading one of his Civil War books and my mother was sewing. She smiled at me and said, "Have a good time coasting, dear?"

I said I sure did and felt pretty guilty. She pictured me sliding down the Center Street hill and walking up again, over and over, which on the whole would have been a lot more restful. If she'd known what I'd really been doing she'd have had my gizzard for gravy.

When I went to bed I kept seeing that car coming at me, big as a battleship and as menacing, and kept thinking how unbelievably lucky I'd been. If I'd hit that curb a couple feet farther along I'd have been mashed like an ant you step on. Miss Wilson would have been right; I wouldn't be around for the end of the world.

CHAPTER

13

Artist on the Job

I DIDN'T SPEND a lot of time brooding about it, but now and then in the next day or so I'd find myself smack in the middle of those last wild and scary minutes behind the big Packard. I'd see it coming at me like a ship on a tidal wave, I'd hear the slap-thunk of the wheel against the curb close to my head, and my stomach would fill up with cold quivery Jell-O.

It didn't occur to me until the second, or maybe third, time I relived that moment, but I suddenly realized that not once during the whole experience did I really believe I was going to get killed or even hurt. Scared, yes. But about to get killed? No.

So my father was right about that, too: people can't really believe they're going to stop living. Was that what I felt about the end of the world? Was it going to take everybody else and leave *me*? Doing what? Floating around in space looking for a nice new planet to come along and take me aboard? Why not me and Judy Felton?

There was sure a lot more thinking to be done

before I could nail down once and for all what I really believed, or didn't believe, was destined to happen on May Day.

On Wednesday I got a welcome surprise. When I got home from school I made myself a peanut butter sandwich and while I was eating it at the breakfast table and reading the funnies in the morning paper I heard Felice come in. She called out, "Mother!"

"Not home yet," I hollered. "Delphian Society, I think."

She came far enough into the kitchen to see me. "It's you I want anyway. When you get through feeding your face come up to my room. Got something to show you."

It had to be something about the poster, so I nearly choked myself on the last bite of sandwich, got it down with a swig of milk, and went on up. She was at her drawing board taping down a good-sized sheet of paper. "Take a look," she said. Plain to see she was pleased about it.

I got behind her and looked. It was the preliminary sketch and it hit me like a sunrise over the prairie. After I'd studied it long enough to really *see* the details, I said, "Gee, Felice . . . wow! . . . it's a *knockout*! I *knew* you'd think up some terrific stuff!"

"Nothing to what it'll look like on the illustration board," she said, trying to sound modest.

I went on looking, really bowled over. Anybody would have been, unless they were Michelangelo or one of those guys. The sheet was divided horizontally into three big blocks of deep color—red, green, and blue—and the lettering was dead white. All the important words—like Authors and Highlight Liter-

ARY EDITION and PUBLICATION had diagonal lemon-yellow stripes that made them fairly sizzle against those brilliant backgrounds. Then, all around the edge, in a wide yellow border, she'd drawn cartoons in black—two series of them, starting at the top center and ending at center bottom. At the top were a boy and a girl, back to back—the girl at a desk biting a pencil, the boy scratching his head in front of a typewriter. In the next pictures on either side they both had light bulbs in bubbles over their heads, and in the next ones, going down the sides, they were both writing furiously. At the lower corners they were still writing, with big stacks of paper piling up. And at the bottom center, facing each other with big smiles, they were dropping their manuscripts into the Entries box.

Felice said, "On the poster everything will be four times the size you're looking at, and the colors will be better. Those letters will really show up."

I said I could hardly wait—and I meant it—to see the finished product. She said, "I worked on the big one during art class and study hall and lunch period, so it's half done, maybe more. All the lettering's in, and about a third of the drawings. So if I take the same time tomorrow it'll be finished in time for you to take it to school on Friday."

I tried to tell her how impressed I was—her working so hard and going without lunches and everything—but what I said sounded pretty feeble. Didn't much matter; she was hardly listening. "I got interested," she said. "When I do that I don't notice how much work it is." I could tell she wasn't really looking at me, but through me and beyond, half smiling.

I said, "Gee, if I'd known it would be all that work

I'd have been scared to ask you." That sounded feeble too. I wanted to tell her I'd do the dishes by myself for a whole week, but couldn't quite bring myself to say the words.

Next day after school I was ready and waiting when Felice got home. Didn't even fix myself a snack. I'd been thinking about the poster all day, except when I got sidetracked during history class. The guy at the desk behind me is a simp named Ralph Stottlemeyer. He'd no sooner sat down than he poked me in the back, gave me this wiseacre grin, and said, "Hey Walden! You sure must have something that don't show!"

I said, "What're you talking about?"

"*I* saw you yesterday, cuddling up in a doorway with Judy Felton!"

This naturally burned me up and I said, "We weren't *cuddling*, dummy, we were *talking*. And try minding your own stupid business!"

He just grinned even more infuriatingly. "Walden the ladies' man! Tim the sheik!"

I had to swallow what I would have said next because right then Mrs. Wemble called the class to order. It didn't take me long to cool off, thinking things over. Ladies' man—nobody had ever called me that before, no reason to. No reason to now either, but I had to admit I sort of liked the sound of it. Ralph was the kind of guy who was sure to blab, and if it got blabbed that I was a ladies' man it just might do me more good than harm. If nothing else, it might give me a little more confidence in the girl department.

Felice came home in somebody's auto, a new LaSalle about the size of a Pullman car. Since I was watching for her I saw it roll up the drive and let her out. She turned around and somebody handed the poster out, wrapped this time in pinkish paper that must have come from the art class.

She brought it in, unwrapped it carefully, and set it on the narrow table at the foot of the stairs. "*Tadada*da *ta*da!" Trumpets.

Well, it was hard to believe but it looked ten times as good as the preliminary. Hard to believe too that anything that good could have been done by a person as young as Felice. I just kept looking, not knowing what to say, and in a minute she said, "You want to pay me now or owe me?"

I looked at her pretty closely to make sure she was really kidding, then I said, "Jeepers—I'll have to owe you for a long, long time if I'm going to pay what that's worth!"

Now she smiled a little. "I'll charge it to experience. I got all fired up and enjoyed myself doing it, so I guess we're even." She started to turn toward the stairs, then paused and added, "When you're finished with it, give it back to me. That is, if it's not all bent and scarred up. I can put it in my portfolio."

I must have looked as blank as I felt because she said, a little impatiently, "Collection of stuff I'm proud of—to show people who might want to hire me for something."

Not for the first time I had to admit Felice was, as Grampa often said, "A young lady with a head on her shoulders."

When she went upstairs I took the poster to the dining room and propped it up in front of the mirror in the big oak sideboard for everyone to see. They all praised it, including Uncle Art who for once didn't speak jokingly. "Time's coming," he said, "when the art world will be saying, 'Miss Walden, name your price!'"

A few seconds after he'd said it I wished he hadn't, because I suddenly remembered that that time wasn't going to come. But on the other hand, tomorrow *was.*

That evening I phoned Carl Simons and told him I'd be bringing the poster to school. He whistled into the phone and said, "No kidding? That sister of yours must be a ball of fire!"

I said that was no lie and he told me he'd call a committee meeting for tomorrow right after school in Mr. Fairborn's room. "We'll have an unveiling," he said.

And that's what happened. In the morning I wrapped the poster up again just the way it had been and got it to school without an accident. (There was no wind at all.) I knew my locker wouldn't hold it so I went to the front office and arranged to leave it in a safe place there.

By the time I'd retrieved it after the last class and got to Mr. Fairborn's room (he was faculty advisor for the *Highlight*) all the others were there and Carl announced that the business of the meeting was to accept or not accept the poster offered by Tim Walden. "So the floor's yours, Tim. Let's get on with the unveiling."

I didn't have any doubt about its acceptance but all the same I felt a little stage fright when I set the poster up on the ledge at the bottom of the blackboard, facing backwards, and started untying the string. The paper seemed to make an unholy racket as I worked it off the illustration board and smoothed it out against the blackboard.

Then I said, "Okay . . . here goes!" and quickly turned the board around and stepped away.

The reaction was even better than I'd expected. First there was a stunned silence, then one gasp and exclamation after another. Of course the voice I heard above all the rest was the one I wanted to hear. "Ohhhh, *dreamy!*" Judy said.

"Remarkable," said Mr. Fairborn. "Remarkable! I understand your sister did it?"

"Yes, sir. On illustration board, with poster paint." Tim Walden, art expert.

"Extremely talented girl, your sister."

"Runs in the family," I said, and added that if the poster was approved I'd put it up on the bulletin board after the meeting. *The* bulletin board meant the huge one in the main hall right outside the office.

Carl said, "I'll go out on a limb and say this poster's approved by unanimous vote. Tim, why don't you go put it up right now? There are still people in the building. They'll see it and the word will start getting around."

I did it, feeling a little annoyed that he hadn't offered me some help—namely Judy's. Once I'd got it up, using some thumbtacks I got from the office, I took a look at it from across the hall. It looked terrific, really grabbed your attention, and before I turned the corner on the way back to the meeting room I looked over my shoulder and saw a group gathered in front of it already.

When I reported that to the committee, Carl said,

"Just what I figured. Entries will be coming in any day. I'll go right to the office from here and arrange for a box on the counter, then I'll tack a note under the poster saying to put entries in it. Tim, how about you check the box every day, and sort of screen them, then divvy 'em up among us. Short stories to Liza, since that's her specialty. Poetry to Judy, and Joe and I'll take the articles and other stuff, and—"

"And I'll help with the poetry," I said, casual-like, but fast.

"Yeah, good," said Carl. "'Cause there'll probably be more of that than anything else."

Now I wasn't annoyed at Carl anymore, and I hoped there'd be dozens of poems, and that Judy would need a second opinion on every one of them. I wished there were some entries in already, but there couldn't be any before next week, and I had the weekend to get through.

Saturday of course meant boxing lesson and when I got to the Y I had to take a really big jump from daydreams of reading poetry with Judy Felton in some secluded spot to getting into my smelly gym trunks and gloves that were even smellier—as if they'd been in constant use since John L. Sullivan's day.

In the gym we found The Kid, as we'd taken to calling him, down on the floor doing fast push-ups, making it look as easy as breathing. Getting up, he said, "A'right, fellas, today we're gonna mix it up a little, do some real sparring, so you better get to warming up. Push-ups first. Twenny-five of 'em. 'Member and keep yer body straight. Don't wanna see no butts up in the air." He dropped into the same position. "'Kay, here we go . . . one . . . two . . . three . . . four. . . ."

When we got to twenty-five and stopped, I sagged onto the floor like a sack of cement and figured I was about as warmed up as I wanted to get. The Kid held a stopwatch. "'Kay, we're gonna do one-minute rounds. Somebody din't show up today so we got a even number, leavin' me out of it."

He paired us off with the you-an'-you method, and told each pair to stand facing each other. I was paired with a tow-headed guy about my size called Jeeter. We stood there trading dim smiles to show we didn't have any very violent intentions. The Kid went on. "When I yell 'Bong!' the round starts. Another bong and it's over. Now, we're gonna mix it up but we ain't out to hurt one another. Don't wanna see nobody throw a haymaker. 'Kay . . . get set . . . Bong!"

Jeeter and I flailed away at each other for a few seconds like a couple of railroad semaphores until The Kid raised his voice again. "Hey Tim . . . you and Whosit . . . slow it down! You ain't choppin' trees, yer boxin'! *Use* them punches, don't waste 'em. You only got just so many!"

Nothing like being made fun of in public. Jeeter and I both slowed down and started paying attention to what we'd been taught. Even so, I'd never known a minute to last so long.

Round Two came, then Round Three, which lasted about an hour, at the end of which we all collapsed as if we'd been machine-gunned.

The Kid didn't join us in the shower, not having exercised much but his mouth. But he did stick his head in and yell, "Last thing you do, turn them showers *cold*. Go outside in this weather all warmed up, you'll catch new*mon*ya! Do like I say, now, or you'll be sorry!"

I managed to avoid pneumonia but all the way home on the streetcar I couldn't think about anything much except how pooped I was. And then a funny thing happened after dinner. I was reading a book that had fighting in it—with swords, not fists—and I found myself thinking about the boxing lesson and realized I wasn't tired anymore and didn't hurt anywhere. The startling thing was that I actually remembered those three rounds with *pleasure*. I'd *enjoyed* it. Enjoyed landing punches and standing a few in return. I even remembered the things Kid McClusky had said, including "You gotta keep workin' at it."

I've never been hypnotized, but it must be something like that. I closed the book as if a voice were telling me to, went down to the coal room, and whacked away at the punching bag for about fifteen minutes. If I was getting even a little bit good at boxing, I wanted to get *better*.

The best part of it was that suddenly it occurred to me that when the chips were down I might stand a chance against Dunk Bolander. Maybe I couldn't whip him, but at least I could put up a fight—whether the world really ended or not.

CHAPTER
14

A Nice Time on the Hill

AS EXPECTED THERE was nothing in the *Highlight* box on Monday, but I looked three times anyway, praying for poetry. On Tuesday something was there, but it was a story by a quiet guy I didn't know very well. Darrell Zimmer. It was called "Crabapple for the Teacher" and it was really funny. I marked it as a leading contender before passing it on to Liza.

On Wednesday there were three entries, two poems and one story. I didn't take time even to glance at them but hotfooted it down the hall toward the room where Judy's next class would be. I caught her in the hall and handed her the two sheets. "Your first customers," I said, ready for cries of joy and a dazzling smile.

What I got was a comical expression of pain and an "Oh, *dear!*"

"Gee," I said. "I thought you'd be glad."

"Well, I *should* be, but . . ." She put a hand on my arm, and for the second time I found myself being steered out of the middle and over to the side of the corridor. I couldn't stop a thought that flickered momentarily at the back of my head: Tim the ladies' man, at it again.

Now she gave me a worried look and said, "It's not that I don't want to do this, Tim, it's just that I don't feel, well, *qualified*. It's like pretending to be something I'm not."

"But Carl said—"

"I know what he said. But the fact is, I *like* poetry—I read it and sometimes I try to *write* it—but that doesn't mean I should be a judge of other people's work. Why don't you get somebody else for this? Maybe Liza—"

"No!" The word just exploded out of me, and it was no phony ladies' man talking, it was Tim Walden trying to keep his big chance from going down the drain. Self-preservation. "No, Judy," I went on. "You're the best we've got. Carl knew that or he wouldn't have suggested you. Gosh, we haven't got *any* high-powered literary critics in eighth grade! Look at me—I got appointed because I read a lot and sometimes Miss Wilson reads my papers to the class; so I'm no critic either, but both of us—you and me—are as good as we've got."

Judy said "But" two or three times but I just kept going, only a little louder. "Tell you what," I said next. "You read these, then we'll get together and *I'll* read 'em, then we'll swap opinions, and right away it'll be clear that you know more about poetry than I do, so—"

Suddenly she smiled. "Tim Walden, you'll *have* to be a *lawyer*! You could talk a jury into turning an ax-murderer loose!"

"Then you'll do it?"

She smiled again and I enjoyed it even more than the first time. "I'll have to, won't I, or you'll keep lecturing me until I'm way late for history class."

I said, "Sorry—forgot about the time."

She looked at me, not smiling, just sort of twinkling. "You're not a *bit* sorry," she said, slipping the two poems into her notebook. "So where shall we have this meeting?"

I thought fast. "Cafeteria. Right after last period."

She nodded, waggled a set of fingers at me, and set off down the hall. I watched her go, enjoying the sight, until suddenly the bell clanged and I whirled and ran like an antelope for Algebra.

After I got home from school I wandered into the kitchen where my mother was putting something into the oven. Straightening up, she looked at me and said, "Late, aren't you?"

I nodded. "Working on *Highlight* stuff."

She went on looking at me. "It must have been very enjoyable work."

Jarred out of my trance, I said, "What do you mean?"

"Just that you looked rather pleased with yourself. In a dreamy sort of way."

It's supernatural, the way my mother can read my mind. I hurried to throw up a smokescreen. "Oh. Well, it's pretty interesting, reading and discussing manuscripts, making literary judgments, things like that."

"I'm sure it is," she said.

Well, I was sure too. We'd spent the better part of half an hour, Judy and I, making literary judgments, although I'd had a hard time keeping my mind on the poems. We read them to ourselves, then she had read them both aloud, which made them sound a lot better than they had before. I managed to prove to her that she was a much better poetry critic than I was. Not very hard to do, since it was true. But I volunteered to discuss future entries at any time. Generous to a fault.

Now I ordered my face to quit looking pleased and dreamy and said, "Well, guess I'd better get at my homework. I mentioned that Ed and I were going sliding after dinner, didn't I?"

I was almost out the door on that line when my mother startled me, saying, "Feeling all right, are you?"

"Well, sure," I said. "Why d'you ask?"

"No sandwich," she said. "No cinnamon toast."

"Oh," I said, and added with a careless laugh—*ha ha ha*—"not hungry. Somebody gave me half a candy bar." It was true. Judy had shared hers with me, which I preferred to believe she wouldn't have done with just *anybody*.

My mother didn't offer any more questions and I escaped to my room. I was sure going to have to keep track of what my face was doing.

When dinner was over I zipped through my part of the cleanup so fast that Felice said, "Ease up—you're not going to get a promotion!"

I said, "Ed'll be here pretty soon. We're going sliding."

"Over on Center Street?"

"Yep," I said, not suspecting anything.

"Gee," Felice said. "That sounds like fun. Okay if I come along?"

Well, if my teeth had been false they'd have fallen

out. I think I made a kind of strangling noise before forcing out some words. "Uh . . . sure. That'd be . . . uh . . . *keen*."

Suddenly she broke into a laugh. "Scared you, didn't I? Ohhh, you should have seen your face! Of *course* I'm not going to come along and spoil your . . . whatever it is you kids are up to."

I couldn't think of anything useful to say so I kept quiet, but three questions kept chasing one another around in my head: What did Felice know? How did she know it? Would she ever get mad enough at me to tell my folks? In the end I calmed myself down by deciding she'd never do that, no matter how mad she might get. She was no snitch.

It was a big relief to hear Ed's whistle outside at 7:20 by the kitchen clock just as I was putting away the last of the dishes. So far it had been a pretty wearing day, what with the strain of promoting myself during two separate face-to-face meetings with Judy Felton, then having my mind looked into by my mother and sister in turn. But all that slid into the background when Ed and I set out on our second attempt to hitch around the course under the set rules. With Ed everything was free and easy. I didn't have to work myself into a lather trying to make the right impression. I wouldn't have to think up convincing ways of avoiding the truth without actually lying to my mother.

I wanted to brag to Ed about my progress with Judy, but the whole story would take too long. So I boiled it down to saying I'd been seeing a lot of her and thought she was getting to like me pretty well.

I should have known better. He said, "Great! When does the kissing begin?"

"Don't be a dope!" I said. "It takes time to work up to that point. Take it slow, wait for the right moment."

Under the street light at the Iola corner he shook his head pityingly. "What you need is . . . They give kissing lessons down there at the Y?"

"Boy, you're a real comedian!" At that point we flopped down on our sleds for the easy glide down to our starting point so we couldn't talk for a while, which was a good thing.

Down by the drugstore we went into our usual act. Our sleds on the ground, we were a couple of kids leaning on a power pole, swapping lies. There were several cars at the curb facing south and we kept an eye on them. After a few minutes a middle-aged couple came out of Borrusch's and headed for a 1926 Reo. They were having an argument. I heard him say, "Now, hold your damn horses, Edith—what makes you think I'd do a thing like that?"

We didn't care who won the argument, just hoped they'd go clear to Ingersoll while they had it. When they got in, slamming the daylights out of both doors, we snatched up the sleds and scuttled in an awkward crouch toward the car. We tailed on—Ed on the right, me on the left as usual. It was ten till eight, judging from the last time I'd peered at the clock through Borrusch's window.

The starter ground so I ducked and shut my eyes, waiting for the first smoky blast of exhaust from the tailpipe. I got it, then came the familiar drag on my right arm and we were moving. The snow was exactly right, almost as slick as ice but not as hard. The driver accelerated—and here came that feeling of flying again.

We didn't fly long. At Pleasant Street the car slowed and turned left, which wouldn't take us where we wanted to go, so we dropped off and dug our toes in. I said "Nuts!", Ed said "Rats!", and we picked up our sleds and headed back where we'd come from. We could easily have walked on to Ingersoll, but that was three long blocks and the rules only allowed us one for walking, so we had to start over.

Our next hitch, a Chevy coupe, was hardly a hitch at all. It turned right at Center and we had to go back again. Ed said disgustedly, "Holy catfish—at this rate we'll be all night!"

I said, "This kind of luck has got to change."

For once I was right. On the next try, a new Buick sedan—with chains—zipped us straight to Ingersoll, turned right, and pulled to the curb in front of Kaufman's grocery. We scrambled for the sidewalk and pulled to the curb before the driver, a tall fellow in a red plaid mackinaw, came striding around the car and on into the store. I doubt if he even noticed that the two kids standing there with sleds hadn't been there when he pulled up. Just as well.

Ed said, "I guess he's after something they didn't have at Piggly Wiggly."

If so, he must have found it because in a minute he came out carrying a small sack. We had backed off a-ways and were pretending we weren't there when he came stalking right up to us. We looked up, plenty startled. His face was as lean as the rest of him and sort of good-looking in a rugged way. Like Tom Mix. He looked us over while we stood there like a couple of toadstools with faces. Then he said in a deep voice that matched his looks, "You boys hitching rides?"

Ed and I threw scared looks at each other. Nothing like this had ever happened before. Ed didn't show any sign of being able to talk, so I said, "Y-yessir." I knew a lie wouldn't work.

"Dangerous thing to do. You know that." It wasn't a question. Statement of fact.

"I—I guess so."

"You *guess* so. If you're half as bright as you look you know damn well it is."

Even if I'd wanted to I couldn't argue, not after the near smash last time. It didn't seem useful to say anything at all. His gaze shifted over to Ed. "What about you? You know it too?"

Ed looked at me. Some help I was going to be! He said the same thing I had. "Y-yessir."

The man tucked his sack under one arm and shoved his hands into the mackinaw pockets. "So you both know it and you do it anyway." I just nodded a little. "And you'll go right on doing it?"

I started feeling a little resentful. This guy didn't have any right to lecture me, as if he'd been my father. Even if he was saying about what my father *would* have said.

"Well, sir," I said, "I guess that's right."

He shook his head then, giving up on us, turned and took a couple of strides toward his car, then swung around, stared toward us, and said, "Well, better me than a lot of drivers I've seen. Where you headed?"

I was too amazed to say anything at all for a second or two. Ed recovered quicker. "Out Ingersoll to Polk," he said. "Then north to—"

"Never mind north; I'll be going beyond Polk."

That's all he said. Just turned again and got into the

Buick while Ed and I stood there looking questions at each other. When the car started up he said, "Why not?" So we did, and in about four minutes we flashed past Forty-fourth Street. When he slowed down for Polk, which is a boulevard, we bailed out and coasted to a stop right at the corner. When the car pulled away, heading west, the guy gave two quick honks on the horn, which amazed us all over again. We sat on our sleds for a couple of minutes wondering aloud what had made that man do what he'd done. We talked about it later on other occasions and never did figure him out. We agreed, though, that what he'd said worried us some. We knew hitching could be dangerous; we'd found that out the hard way. We also knew we had no intention of stopping, which didn't exactly make us the brightest people in the world. It wasn't comfortable. But on the other hand, if there wasn't going to be another winter it wouldn't matter whether we intended to go on with it or not.

After one car had turned right off Ingersoll while we just stared at it, we quit working our mouths and got our brains into the game, so the next car to make the turn picked up a couple of passengers. This one was a Lincoln, a really classy car.

Our luck was still in. There were five streets the car could have turned on between there and Kingman, but it didn't even pause. When it slowed at Kingman I thought sure it was going to turn. It never pays to outguess a driver, so we hung on, and after a near stop at Kingman it sailed on across and picked up speed. We were on our way to University.

At that intersection we got held up, which was worrisome because we could run out of time without knowing it. We knew there was a drugstore on one corner, and a couple of shops, but by this time they'd all closed for the night. No lighted windows, no cars at the curb. Nothing to do but wait for a car to turn right off Polk.

Finally, an old Model-T closed coupe came along. It sits up high and has bigger windows than newer cars. We made our dash, latched on, the car moved forward, and we thought we were on our way when suddenly it stopped, a door opened, and some guy yelled at us to get off or he'd come back there and beat our ears in.

Well, we could take a hint, so we got off and sauntered away until he passed out of sight around the corner. Then we got back in position again. The next car that passed hugged the center island and turned left after stopping. Then it seemed forever until the next one came. It was a Kissel Straight-8 Speedster, low slung and sleek but with its top up so that there was only a narrow, stretched-out window in back. This time we made it unseen and unyelled at and went zipping east on University.

From there it was easy as falling off a log. With just one more hitch after that we made it to Thirty-fifth, and nothing bad had happened the whole evening, except for getting lectured once and yelled at after that. And we hadn't even *seen* a high school guy driving.

Thirty-fifth isn't a main thoroughfare like the others, but it carries enough traffic to give you a chance, and after about ten minutes we caught a Dodge sedan heading south. It crossed Cottage Grove but turned east on Kingman, so we let go and coasted on as far as momentum could take us, which was about half a block from home. It still wasn't time to celebrate, because we didn't know what time it was.

"My house!" I said, and we ran the rest of the way as fast as anybody could while lugging a five-foot sled. We dumped the sleds in the front yard, stumbled in through the side door, up the steps, into the kitchen, and looked at the clock on top of the stove. It said 8:58. Two minutes to spare!

We couldn't cheer even though we felt like yelling our heads off, so we grinned like panting dogs, shook hands violently, and said in strangled whispers, "We did it! We made it!"

About then my father called from the front room where we'd already heard voices. "What's the matter, you two—cops after you?"

Ed and I went on grinning and I hollered back, "No cops. We're pursued by awful hunger pangs. Are there any cookies?"

This put the ball in my mother's court and she took a turn at hollering. "Usual place—and there's a little cake left. There's milk or ginger ale in the refrigerator!"

I was about to say thanks when her voice came again, closer now, and I heard her quick footsteps. "Wait a minute, I've got another idea."

Seconds later she came through the doorway and stopped, staring at our feet. "For heaven's sake, boys, you know better than to come in the house with wet galoshes! Go get them off, then come back and wipe up this mess! Hop to it!"

We hopped, but not even a scolding could cool us down much, so we didn't mind the cleaning up at all and when we'd finished my mother said, "What I was about to ask was how would you like some hot cocoa instead of cold drinks?"

While we ate cake and cookies and waited for the marshmallows to melt down just right into the cocoa we rehashed the whole evening in low voices while my folks got on with the bridge game they'd been playing while we were gone. Naturally the subject came up of the man who'd lectured us.

"You think he's right?" Ed said. "You know, that we're dummies to go on hitching rides?"

I thought about it and said, "Maybe. But look at it this way. Of all the times we've done it we only had that one close shave. Well . . . *two*. Tonight it was a regular tea party."

He nodded. "We've just got to be careful and never break our own rules."

That made us feel better, at least for the time being. But I didn't forget that man. He was one who knew how to make an impression. I thought about him again after Ed had gone home and I'd gone into the front room where the bridge game was going on. I thought of him because my mother looked up and said, "Have a nice time sliding, did you?" I said we sure did, and heard the man saying, "If you're half as bright as you look . . ." And here I was, pulling the wool over my mother's eyes and knowing I'd do it again.

There wasn't much relief to be got by reminding myself that after this winter was over I'd never be able to do it again anyway. I could have thought of a lot of things more cheerful than that.

CHAPTER

15

Sweet Victory

AS THE DAYS went by I managed pretty well, with determination and strength of character, to nail the lid down on my conscience so it wouldn't get loose and ruin my fun. Commonsense was on my side too. It stood to reason that if this was the last winter there would ever be, I'd be crazy to let it go to waste.

Even Ed's conscience was giving him a little trouble, though not more than he could stand, so we went hitching quite a few more times while the snow lasted without getting into any real trouble—except once.

There had been a few sunny days but the temperature stayed well down in the teens and colder than that at night, so we weren't worried much about thawing. We did hit a few spots where our sled runners cut through to the pavement, mainly at intersections, which got traffic going two ways, or on south-facing slopes that got more sun than most places.

Each time it meant only a second's drag on the arm and hand holding the car bumper. Not even as scary as hitting a manhole cover. These were always bare because of the heat down below, and we were used to handling them.

We'd caught a ride at Twenty-sixth and Forest going west, figuring that with luck we'd make it to Forty-second on Forest and then head back on Kingman. Like a lot of plans, it didn't work out. The driver of the Willys-Knight sedan turned right on Thirtieth, heading north. I looked over at Ed and he nodded, so we stayed on.

We had a good ride, just fast enough to be exciting, and the driver wasn't doing anything foolish, but pretty soon after we'd crossed Hickman Avenue I began wondering what we ought to do. Not too far ahead was the Urbandale carline, and beyond that we'd be practically out in the country where there'd be hardly any intersections for catching new rides.

I needn't have worried because we never got that far. Just after we crossed New York Street, I felt a tug on my arm that meant we were starting up an incline. I tightened my grip. About two seconds later the tug turned into a scary drag. Beneath me there was bare pavement and both sleds were throwing sparks like axes on grindstones. The sun had got at that slope, melted the snow, and dried the pavement. In a flash I knew I'd have to let go—either that or get yanked clear off the sled. Automatically I took a quick look to the rear and nearly fainted. There was a pair of headlights back of us, too close for comfort. It was hold on and get yanked off or let go and get run over. Some choice. Actually it wasn't a choice at all; my arm wouldn't stand another second of that awful drag, and already my chest was inching forward on the sled.

I let go and instantly the sled stopped as if it had hit a stone wall. From the corner of my eye I saw Ed do the same, and both of us, moving faster than I'd have believed we *could* move, grabbed the sleds and leaped for the right side of the street. The driver behind gave a furious blast on his horn and added to that the squeal of tires as he hit the brakes.

Ed made it first because he was on the right side to begin with, landing on the parking strip in a tangle of arms, legs, and sled. An instant later I did the same and felt the wind of the car's passing and heard a shouted curse from inside the car.

We must have lain there a whole minute at least—watching the tail lights dim and vanish and waiting for our hearts to stop hammering—before either of us said anything.

Ed was first. "Well," he said a little shakily. "We taught *that* guy a lesson—about following too close."

"You know something?" I said. "Maybe it isn't so funny anymore."

"What isn't?"

"Having a close shave and laughing it off."

"Not losing the old nerve, are you?"

"I'm not sure," I said. "Maybe I'm just getting a little smarter."

"Well, get smarter tomorrow. Right now we've got to get home."

He stood up and I did too, feeling pretty wobbly. We walked out in the street and looked at the patch of bare pavement. So, all right, we got by again, because we were quick and skillful. But . . .

We stood there a minute reliving those last awful moments and I couldn't help thinking about the man who'd told us how dumb we were being. Quick and skillful was one thing; stupid was another. I thought about Miss Wilson too, on the subject of not being around for the end of the world. Then I thought about my own argument—that we should go on hitching rides as long as the snow lasted because there'd be no snow again. That argument didn't look so good when I stacked it up against another one—that if I only had a few months left the stupidest thing I could possibly do was spent them in the cemetery.

It took a couple of deep breaths to get started but I finally managed. "Well, we've got to get home tonight for sure. But after that . . . well, maybe hitching rides doesn't make much sense anymore."

Now it was his turn for deep thinking. He did it while we started walking back the way we'd come. About halfway down the block, which was a long one, he said, "You may be right, or you may be wrong, but one thing's sure. I'm not going out hitching by myself."

After that we didn't say much at all. We walked only as far as Hickman where we caught a hitch that took us clear back to the University. From there we got home in just two hitches.

At home I got the usual question. Did I have a nice time out sliding. I said I had.

I'd be sorry, I knew, that my hitching days were over, but maybe it would be worth it to get free of the need to keep pretending that half the truth was the same as all of it.

The ice lasted longer than the snow, so we went on playing hockey until the last possible moment, which was the morning we arrived at Waveland—second week of March, I think—to find the hockey area closed off by signs saying DANGER—NO SKATING BEYOND THIS POINT. Some guys were out there anyway, finding out what it felt like to glide over ice that sank beneath you and rose up again behind. Ed and I already knew from scary experience.

All this time I'd been working on the *Highlight* and having little poetry sessions with Judy during which I caught some of her enthusiasm so that poetry was coming to mean more than just a chance to be with her. Also I'd gone on working out on the punching bag and got so I could do a pretty fair imitation of Kid McClusky's performance. During lessons I'd been matched with every guy in the class, and while I hadn't done anything very spectacular I'd given as good as I'd got, sometimes a little better—with the exception of one guy with arms as long as an ape's who kept jabbing me dizzy until I learned to get in under it and connect with a few good lefts to the belly.

But the more I improved the more I wondered if I could really ever learn *enough*. Once I got into a fight with Dunk Bolander, would all the skill I was learning do anything but slow him down a little on his way to beating me to a pulp? Maybe picking a fight with him, which was what I might have to do, would be as dumb as risking my neck on a sled.

It took me about four seconds to recognize that idea for what it was: an easy out, a sorry excuse for not doing what needed to be done. Fighting Dunk was dangerous but I had to do it or arrive at the end of the world knowing I didn't have enough guts to stick up for myself.

He hadn't given me any trouble for quite a while

now. Once, he'd spotted me coming up the front steps to the Y and came charging down pretending not to see me, just to find out if I'd get out of the way. I did and hated myself, of course, but for once I didn't cool off and start hoping the whole thing would blow over. Next time there'd be no stepping aside, no matter what.

The reason our paths didn't cross much was that he never came on Saturdays and for quite a while I'd been too busy to go on weekdays the way I used to. But I was there all right on April fourteenth when the whole situation blew up like a fireworks factory.

I remember the date because it was the day before our *Highlight* deadline when everything had to be ready to go off to the printer. I'd finished my part of it the day before. That was to collect the last of the winning manuscripts from Betty Jo Kaplan, the only committee member who could type. Before giving them to her I'd corrected the originals, some of which I'd read four or five times during the selection process. This time I was looking mainly for spelling and punctuation mistakes; and when I got them back from Betty Jo I had to go over them once more for typographical errors she might have made. Then I turned them over to Carl Simons who would take them to the printing office along with the rest of the things—layout sheets, pictures and captions, stuff like that.

With that out of the way I felt "free as a flea on a hound dog," as Grampa always put it, so right after school on the fourteenth I took the streetcar down as close as it came to the Y. I left my books at the desk, which was manned that day by a college guy they call

Duke, who works for his room at the Y and goes to Drake University.

The pingpong table was in use and so were the two pool tables, but the billiard table, over closest to the windows, was being used by a guy named Ted, who was in the boxing class. He was fooling around, practicing three-cushion shots. I watched for a minute or two and saw he was pretty good—better than I was, probably—but I asked him anyway if he needed an opponent. He said sure, so I took a cue from the rack between the big windows, and we got started.

I guess I like pool better than billiards because sometimes you can slam the cue ball into a cluster and get lucky, but in billiards luck doesn't count for much. It's about ninety-nine percent skill. You've got to have an eye for angles that's like some kind of machine. If you're off by the width of a fly's hind leg you miss your shot. It takes a lot of concentration.

That's why I wasn't much aware of what was going on at the next table, except as background noise, and didn't realize that the two guys playing pool had given way to two others. But I sure knew it the second a voice broke what was an unusual moment of silence in that room.

"Well, if it ain't the new Jack Dempsey! Got any big fights lined up? I don't wanna miss the broadcast."

No mistaking that cobblestone voice with the built-in sneer. I forced myself to turn slow and easy instead of flipping around like a mechanical toy. I tried to pretend I thought this was just ordinary kidding around and said, "It'll be in all the papers."

He proved he could put a sneer even into a grunt but didn't say anything else and I thought maybe my snappy comeback had shut him up. I turned back when Ted said from the other side of our table, "It's all yours; I missed my shot."

I bent over, sizing up the angles for a two-cushion shot, knowing my concentration was smashed to pieces now and I was sure to make a mess of it. But I had to try, so I lined up on the cue ball and the spot I was aiming for on the first cushion, studied it for another second or two, and started the forward stroke with the cue.

My cue tip never came near the ball; it jabbed instead into the table's green felt cover almost hard enough to gouge a hole in it. I'd suddenly taken a poke by a hard object in the middle of my bent-over rear end. I knew instantly what had happened: Dunk Bolander had watched for the crucial moment and goosed me with a pool cue! I whirled, saw him slouching there at the corner of the next table, cue stick held loosely in right hand, smirk firmly in place.

Without even a thought I launched myself at him like a projectile and crashed into him with my right shoulder. His cue flipped from his hand and slapped the linoleum floor with a crack like an air rifle's.

My momentum sent him staggering backwards until he thumped against the wood-paneled wall, and I went right along with him, throwing a whirlwind of punches, every one of which hit him somewhere. The *where* didn't matter to me so long as I hit him—hurt him—punished him. And I was hurting him all right; I could tell by the grunts he was letting out, and every grunt was beautiful music to me.

I guess it was Uncle Art who once said "You can't fight a crazy man" and that's what I was right then—

crazy. I was beyond reason, beyond fear, beyond pain. I was ready to keep on slugging as long as I had strength to raise my fists or stay on my feet. It was true too, that he couldn't fight me. All he managed to do finally was to get his arms up and cover his face. He was a little late about it; I'd already been startled by a rush of blood from his nose, spreading to his mouth and chin.

Never in the whole time did I remember anything I'd learned in all those boxing classes. Good thing too; if I'd got into the stance for the jab-punch-counter-punch routine he'd have had time to get set too and probably would have knocked me silly. What I was doing had no science to it, nothing but an explosion of rage damped down over a period of months but still building and building inside, and what lit my fuse now would have lit anybody's.

I don't know how long I went on flailing away like a robot gone wild—maybe no more than a minute—but all of a sudden I was aware of voices and heavy footsteps. A pair of hands grabbed me from behind, pinned my arms to my sides, and a voice right in my ear was saying, "Stop! *Hold* it! You trying to *kill* him?" It was the college guy, Duke. I didn't even try to resist; there was no strength left in my arms and I was gasping for air as if I'd been underwater for five minutes. "Jeez, kid," said the voice in my ear. "Can't you see he's had enough? What started this anyway?"

I couldn't have answered anything that took more wind than a yes or a no so I just kept gasping and blowing. Now came another heavy tread, and there was Red Clifford, bear-shaped in his baggy sweatsuit, looking sharply at me, then at Dunk. He said to Duke,

"I'll hold this tiger—you go quick to the first-aid locker, bring one of those kits. Move!"

Duke moved, and Red's big hand closed over my left forearm—unnecessarily because I didn't have a punch left in me. My first thought was, "What do I need with first aid?" Then I looked at Dunk—really *looked* for the first time—and could hardly believe what I saw. He was a mess. Blood everywhere—not just all over his face but his arms were streaked with it and so was the light-colored jersey he was wearing. It took a second, but I figured it out: My fists had got blood from his face and given it back in smeary installments everywhere they'd landed. In addition to all that, his right eye was red and starting to puff up. So was his lower lip. It was hard to believe I'd done all that. Me—peace-loving Tim Walden. I wasn't sorry, though, not for a second.

Duke came trotting back with a square metal box marked with a red cross. Red let go of me, growled, "Back off, everybody," shoved Dunk into a chair, and went to work on his face. I didn't know what to do but wait for my overworked lungs to settle down. I was also beginning to notice that both hands were aching as if I'd been pounding a barrel or something. Two knuckles on my left hand were skinned and sore.

In a minute Red demanded over his shoulder, "How'd this thing get started anyway?"

First to answer—wouldn't you know?—was Dunk Bolander. "He jumped me. No reason, no warning. I didn' even *touch* him."

"That's a lie!" I said.

Red shook his head impatiently. "Not you two! Somebody who witnessed it. Speak right up."

There was a silence, then a voice. Ted, my billiards partner. "Me and Tim were playing billiards. He was making a shot when the other guy reached out his cue and, well, he *goosed* him. No reason I could see. And Tim—he blew up."

Red just nodded and went on working. Dunk let out a couple of loud ouches, and finally Red stood up, saying, "You'll heal. Go to the washroom now and clean up best you can. But don't leave. You'll have to go in and talk to Mr. Crawford." Then he turned to me. "You'll go in after he does."

Well, that wasn't the best news I ever heard. Mr. Crawford is the Y secretary, the man in charge. He's also in charge up at Y Camp, so he was no stranger to me. I'd never been sent into his office before, but I figured that if the price of bloodying Dunk Bolander's nose was a lecturing I'd be glad to pay it.

It didn't turn out quite that way. Mr. Crawford's office is across the front hall from the recreation room. He looked grave when I went in, but then he always does. I sat where he told me to, opposite his desk, and he got right to work. Peering at me over his glasses, he said, "Well, Tim, you've been around the Y long enough to know we don't tolerate fighting except in the gym and under supervision."

I knew that right enough so I just said, "Yessir."

He fiddled around with his fountain pen a little and said, "I understand from Red Clifford that there were certain, uh, mitigating circumstances."

I nodded. "That's the way I look at it, sir."

He went on as if I hadn't opened my mouth. "That you were subjected to an, er, unsavory indignity."

He always uses words like this, so I knew right off

what he was talking about, and I just said, "Yessir, I was."

He made a little tepee with his forefingers and pressed the tip against his lips awhile before going on. "Speaking from many years of experience with boys, and I was a boy once myself"—here he allowed himself a little smile—"I am aware that this particular form of, er, horseplay, distasteful though it may be, is generally regarded as acceptable behavior."

"Not by me, sir."

"That," he said, looking more sorrowful than anything else, "would seem obvious. But wasn't your reaction a bit excessive? In other words, did it justify what you did to the other boy?"

I thought that over, but not quite long enough. I said, "Maybe it wouldn't if this—" I clamped my teeth down on that quick. I didn't believe in snitching, even against Dunk Bolander.

Mr. Crawford looked expectant. "Go on. If this . . . what?"

I went to the bottom of the barrel for an answer. "If this particular thing hadn't made me so mad I couldn't think straight."

He picked it up fast. "That's not what you were going to say, is it?"

"Close enough," I said, shrugging a little.

He looked at me steadily, and somehow a little sadly, as if I'd been a big disappointment to him. "It won't do, Tim. I want the whole truth, not just a piece of it."

I did my best to dummy up, but I was no match for him. Getting the truth out of boys who didn't want to tell it was one of his specialties. In the end I told him about the tormenting, the sneering that I couldn't even begin to account for, and how I'd taken it all because I was afraid not to. I told him about the boxing lessons and my resolution to fight the guy when I got the chance.

When I'd finished he nodded, fiddled some more with his pen, finally nodded again as if he'd come to an agreement with himself, and said, "Well, Timothy, if you were an adult you could be charged with the crime of assault, and upon conviction be subject to imprisonment. However, I am aware that judges take into account the matter of extreme provocation, which to my mind you have successfully pleaded.

"Now you may know that the penalty here for violent behavior is temporary suspension of all Y privileges. But in your case I have decided to, ah . . ." A tiny smile told me: joke coming. ". . . to suspend the suspension."

I relaxed for the first time. What that tangle of words meant was that I was off the hook.

"*However* . . ."

After the *however* came the lecture. I should have known. Personal violence has no place in a Christian environment. . . . One should learn to practice the virtue of self-control. . . . Turn the other cheek. . . . Consider the example of Our Savior, who forgave and blessed those who wronged him. . . . And so forth and so forth. I got the whole sermon, and when he finally ran down I said I'd remember his advice and try to do better. I meant it, too—providing I didn't have to apply any of it to Dunk Bolander.

Bodily I went home on the streetcar, but in spirit I rode on a fluffy cloud. I'd done it! I'd fought my fight and won, even if not in accordance with the rules of the ring, or any other rules. But what if Dunk hadn't had enough? What if he'd try something again? I gave that some careful thought, and the answer was— Let him! I wasn't scared of him anymore. That was the important thing.

And what about turning the other cheek? Thanks all the same, but I'd tried that and all it got me was misery. It worked for Jesus all right, maybe even for Mr. Crawford, but not for me. Even with the end of the world in sight, I had no talent for holiness.

When I got home, still reveling in the taste of triumph, I surprised Uncle Art in the kitchen helping himself to the cookies. He looked at me, cool as a cucumber, stuck a cookie in his mouth, and talked while chomping. "Following your example. You're a bad influence on me."

I was so full of myself I couldn't help giving him a big fat grin. "Better watch out how you talk to me. You could get hurt." I said it out of the side of my mouth and hunched my shoulders, gangster style.

He went on chewing, never taking his eyes off mine, swallowed, and let a grin of his own take over his face. "Well, I'll be a son of a . . . You *did* it! And there's not a mark on you!"

"Plenty on him, though." Barefaced bragging. Couldn't help it.

"Here. Have a cookie and tell me about it."

That was an invitation I couldn't pass up, so I told him the whole incredible story, including the blood and Mr. Crawford and everything.

When I'd finished he said, "Told you, didn't I? Kid with gumption. Wait'll I tell the smokehouse gang!"

That would be my father. Before long the whole household would know they had a slugger in their midst. Right there I began cooling off. Nobody knew any better than I did that I was no slugger. "Well, it wasn't all that great," I said. "Not even a real fight; just me going sort of crazy. I could have done that without a single boxing lesson."

"Well, hey, sport. No sense in raining on your own picnic! The villain's vanquished, isn't he? You did what you set out to do—so enjoy it!"

"Okay," I said. "I will." A thought struck me. "Trouble is, now I've got to pay you for the punching bag."

Uncle Art nodded energetically. "Bet your socks you do. Three and a half bucks. Pay up inside a week or you'll get a fat lip!"

"Watch your mouth, Bo!" I said. There'd never been a time when I felt so good.

CHAPTER

16

Damsel in Distress

I CLUNG TO the memory of my one-sided fight like a baby with its teddy bear, but the first thing that happened next morning shoved it clear out of my head anyway, for the time being. I got an invitation.

Everybody on the *Highlight* staff did. I got mine when Carl Simons and I met in the hall on the way to first period. He just grinned, stuck a note into my shirt pocket, and kept on going. I took time to read it.

"WE MADE IT!" the top line said. Then, "Deadline party Saturday 7:30 P.M. at my house. Revelry—refreshments—games—dancing—backslapping." It was signed "Carl" and the address given below that.

It sounded great—except for one word: Dancing. I could no more dance than a penguin—and come to think of it, that's about what I'd look like if I tried.

Well, I could play games, couldn't I? And I could eat! Two out of three. Good average. So I kept telling myself at unwelcome intervals the rest of the day, but I couldn't get my mind off the dancing. I'd never danced in my life, never even seen any dancing except in the movies, where it was always smooth-looking guys in tuxes doing the Charleston and fox-trot and things like that with glamorous women, usually on crowded nightclub dance floors or the ballrooms of ocean liners. But that was the movies; this was real life.

Well, my imagination, which seldom goes out of its way to be kind to me, offered this picture of Carl's party: all the guys out swirling around the floor with girls in their arms—all except one lone slob crouching in a corner stuffing himself with pie and ice cream and whatever else was available. Maybe he'd be playing a nice game of solitaire at the same time.

When I could manage to shut off the imagination and give my brain a chance, I knew there could hardly be any Hollywood smoothies in my school. Maybe some guys might have taken lessons. Carl was a cinch to know how to dance or he wouldn't have planned it for his party. The girls now, they always seemed to know how. Felice did, and she'd never had any lessons except for ballet when she was a little kid. Maybe they all inherit it from their mothers.

It was what you'd call cold comfort to tell myself that dancing wasn't the only thing I'd never learned to do. Like kissing a girl. And here it was the fifteenth of April. I had two weeks to learn! After the party there'd only be *ten days*. Darn Carl Simons anyway; with just one word he'd wrecked the rest of the week for me. Naturally Judy would know how to dance and would be doing it at the party. But not with me. And how could she be interested in being kissed by a chump who couldn't even dance a step with her?

So all of a sudden it was Desperation Day for sure.

When Felice got home from school I was waiting to open the door for her, wearing the pleading expression I'd been working on for ten minutes.

It wasn't lost on her. In the middle of coming through the door she said, "Oh, *no*! What've I got to do *now*?"

She came on in, put her books down on the stairs—making it clear she was on her way up—and turned to face me. I said, "Felice, could you . . . I mean . . . *will* you teach me how to dance?"

She flung back the wavy hair that tends to fall over one eye. "Good grief!" she said. "I'm just barely good enough to get by. I couldn't *teach* anybody. Thing for you to do is ask Mother."

"Mother! Teach me dancing? But she's—"

I was going to say "too old" and Felice guessed it. "She's thirty-five years old, you nitwit—and she's a good dancer. Ask Dad, ask Uncle Art. She taught them both!"

"She . . . she taught *Dad*?"

She nodded so hard her hair fell over that eye again. "As soon as they started going out together—and he always said he had two right feet, both of them wrong."

I thanked her and said I'd do it, thinking there were certainly a lot of things I didn't know about this family. I found my mother reading a book in the little sitting room that had been my room before we added onto the house a few years back. I told her about the party and said I wouldn't even go to it unless I learned to dance just enough to get by.

She understood right off the bat how desperate I was and put her book down with a little thump. "*Well,* now," she said. "I might do a little better than *that*. We can't have you missing the party just because you don't know the fox-trot! Let's go down to the basement and see what we can do."

My mother put a record on and cranked up the Victrola, but she didn't start it yet. Lecture first. "The fox-trot has nothing to do with foxes, it refers to the dance step, which is very simple. Four-four time with the accent on the first beat: *One*, two, three, four; *one*, two, three, four—like the Indian tom-tom." She demonstrated, humming the tune she was about to play, which was "Yes, Sir, That's My Baby." At the same time she put her feet through the motions without moving very far, coming down extra hard on the heavy beats.

Next she turned the record on and went through the step in time to the music, counting aloud and moving around as if she were really dancing. Then she took the needle off. "That's it—all there is to it. Just keep moving, feeling the rhythm and doing your one-two-three-fours. Simple, isn't it?"

I said, "That's what they told me about algebra."

"No comparison. Come on, let's try it." She stood me by the phonograph and held up her right hand, about shoulder high. "Take hold of my hand with yours—your left—lightly. *Lightly*—remember not to clutch. Now, put your other hand around to the small of my back—firmly but not tight. That's right. Now when the music starts, you listen to the beat, and when the next accented *one* comes you put your left foot forward and a little to the side."

"I'll step on your foot."

"No you won't; it's the girl's job to move right with

you. She'll step back when you step forward. All set?"
She put the needle down and the music started.

That was the way it began. For a while I stumbled around like a blind man in a furniture store, but she kept cranking the machine up and making me start over again until about the tenth time it began to make a little sense and I managed to steer her in a circle, clockwise, all around the space available, and she was encouraging me with little yelps: "Now you got it! Going great!" Once she hauled my left arm back from wherever it was and down to shoulder level. "Break that impulse *now!*" she commanded. "Your elbow is bendable, you know."

I moaned a little. "Too many things to *remember.*"

"Don't let it worry you. They'll become automatic."

"Not by Saturday night!"

What I didn't know was how much practice I was going to get by Saturday night. She might have been Kid McClusky, the way she worked me, drilling away from the time I got home from school each day until she had to quit to fix dinner, then after dinner for as long as we both could stand it.

I got so I knew the words to "Yes, Sir, That's My Baby" as well as I knew "My Country 'Tis of Thee" or "Twinkle, Twinkle, Little Star." I guess she got sick of it too, because she switched to "Bye, Bye, Blackbird" then "Yes, We Have No Bananas." The words to those, I got to thinking, were "Relax—*bend* a little. Stop counting out loud! *Enjoy* yourself—dancing's *fun,* not hard labor!"

She even made Felice take a turn with me now and then so she could stand off to one side and make helpful criticisms. Both of them were pretty free with encouraging words, so when the whole ordeal came to an end with one last session on Saturday afternoon I'd learned more than I'd have believed I could learn in so short a time, and I even felt a faint stirring of confidence that I might get through the evening without setting off screams of laughter.

For once I didn't ask for seconds at dinner but thanked my mother at least four times for taking my turn at the kitchen sink. Then I hurried upstairs to get ready.

I took a bath and slapped on a few drops of Uncle Art's cologne which smelled interesting but not sissified. Then I put on a clean white shirt and a tie my father lent me. He warned me not to get my feet tangled up in it because it had cost five dollars. Put on my suit too. It was blue serge and I'd worn it only three times—two funerals and a wedding.

I pulled a comb through my hair, which is more like wire than anything that ought to grow out of a human head so it usually has things pretty much its own way. After that I took a searching look in the mirror—anyway, as searching as I could stand. No smoothie there. Face: more or less square. Features: somebody wanting to be kind could say, "Quite *regular*." Expression: alert but worried. Upper lip: stiff with slight growth of fuzz visible in a strong light. General impression: about halfway between ugly and handsome. Durable. Good teeth.

Uncle Art had volunteered to chauffeur me. On the way I didn't say much. Too busy entertaining the butterflies in my stomach. No telling how, but Uncle Art seemed to know about the butterflies because after a while he said, quietly for him, "Tell you something. Nobody at this party has got a nickel's worth more experience, or polish, or sophistication than you've got. Where would they have got it? Some may act as if they had, but that's what it is—an act. Anyway, you'll be the only Tim Walden there, and he's quite a guy—take my word for it."

I mumbled something useless, and in a minute he went on. "And now that you ask, girls are the same as boys, even the prettiest. Oh, they catch on to the social graces a little quicker, and make you feel like a clod, but underneath they're just as scared and jumpy as you are. At thirteen it goes with the territory. Guarantee it—I've been there."

I saw the worm in that apple right off and started to say so, but he beat me to it. "I know, I know—I've never been a girl; but I've talked to a good few. They all say the same."

I wasn't about to argue with the kind of experience he's had, and arrived at Carl's house in a state of mind that fell a-ways short of sheer terror. Last thing he said as I got out was, "Stand up in the stirrups, boy—and grab the brass ring!" If he meant what I thought he meant, it was good advice. But like most good advice, probably impossible to follow.

Kid sister was on duty again and led me to this huge basement game room that made ours look like the parts department at Joe's Auto Repair. Walls panelled halfway up, comfortable-looking chairs all over the place, one of those old player pianos against the far wall. Everybody was standing around waiting for the revelry to start.

A quick glance showed me all this, then stuck tight to the figure I was looking for. She had her back to me, talking to another girl. She was wearing a soft green dress made of some thin wool material, clingy, with a belt of gold leather, and those coppery waves of hair stayed in constant motion as she talked animatedly. I'd have bet all the other girls were wishing either she'd stayed home or *they* had.

I might have stood there bug-eyed indefinitely if Carl, who'd been counting noses, called out, "Only thirteen—somebody missing!"

One of the girls said, "Marcy Ruben!" and somebody else said, "Oh, Marcy, she'll be late to her own wedding."

Carl gestured toward a long table with a white cloth on it, next to the player piano. "Punch bowl's open for business. Later on, stuff to eat. Well, let's get started. What say we break the ice with a good old-fashioned kids' game—musical chairs!"

Everybody cheered and while he directed the lining up of a double row of folding chairs in the middle of the room, Marcy Ruben came fluttering in, scattering greetings and apologies around like rose petals, so everybody cheered *her*.

It seemed to me the ice was broken already but we went ahead with musical chairs, making as much racket as a bunch of six-year-olds. Carl stayed by the piano switching the player to start and off again when he judged it was time to scramble for chairs. The tune was the old favorite "Nola," which can't miss when it comes to putting people in a rollicking mood. Right in the middle of it I had my first brilliant idea in quite a while. When the game stopped I made a break for the punch bowl, filled two cups, and made a beeline for where Judy had just sat down in one of the regular chairs. I craftily did this while the other guys were putting the folding chairs back where we'd got them before the game. I handed her a cup and said, "In case of thirst."

She took it with a smile that would have melted a stalactite, thanked me, and drank. "Mmmmm, *good*. I didn't know I was so thirsty!"

"Hot work, musical chairs," I said, swigging a little myself.

"Fun, though—even when you're not seven years old anymore." While I was working out a comment on that she suddenly made a sort of guilty face and burst out, "Well, for goodness sake, Tim, sit down!" She patted the chair next to her. "I'm acting like . . . like you were the *waiter*."

Nudged by one of those Fate things, I said, "Well, I'm at your service." That got me a bubbly little laugh. It may not have been meant to encourage me, but it did—enough to shove me into my next move. Lubricating my throat with a little punch, I said, "Look, if I don't ask you now I'm liable to get trampled in the rush, so . . . so when the dancing starts, may I be the first in line?"

With a moonrise of a smile she said, "When you put it like that, I could hardly refuse, even if I wanted to. Only—why do you think there's going to be a rush?"

I took a quick look around and said, "Well, there are seven guys here, and I think we're all in our right minds."

She rewarded that with another smile, but not until after she'd wrinkled her brow in a puzzled way, as if I'd suddenly started talking Latin or something. Her eyes sort of roamed around my face for a couple of seconds and she said, "You know something? You've changed. I don't know what it is, but something's . . . *different*."

That rocked me back, but I pulled myself together enough to say, "Well, that's good news. Any change has got to be an improvement."

She gave her head a tiny shake. "I'm *serious*. I can't put my finger on it—but it's *there*."

This was too good to be true. She must have been taking more of an interest in me than I had any right to expect. I got my mind up to a boil trying to think of the right thing to say. Finally I came up with, "If you're right, it's . . . well, it's because quite a lot's been happening to me."

Now *she* hesitated a while before saying, "Would you . . . feel like telling me about it?"

Would I? Would I like to be six feet tall and built like Kid McClusky? From the tail of my eye I saw Carl winding up the Victrola again. "Sure I would," I said. "But it's sort of a long story. If . . ." The hesitation was to turn up the fire under my nerve. In the end I took the plunge. "If I could walk you home after the party I could make a stab at telling you."

She left me wobbling on the high wire for at least half a minute before she gave her head a little nod. "I—I'd like that, but . . ." *Always a but*, I thought. "But you know where I live. It's not really far enough for a *long* story."

"I'll talk fast," I said. "And we can walk slow."

The smile came. "All *right*, then."

I felt like a balloon cut loose from the earth, and in a matter of seconds I crashed.

"Hey, you two!" It was Carl, and he went on, "I'm

about to announce the dancing. But first—sorry, Tim—I'll claim the first dance with Judy."

She said, "But Carl, I . . ." and I said, "Hold on, she said she . . ."

But he grabbed her hand and pulled her up from the chair. "Host's privilege!" he said with a grin for both of us, and led her over to the Victrola.

For all I knew there *was* such a thing as host's privilege. Anyway, how could I complain when I'd already hit the jackpot? I'd just skulk around the edges and maneuver to grab Judy for the next one.

I headed for the punch bowl where I could pretend I was busy quenching a raging thirst. Somebody was there ahead of me, probably with the same thing in mind. I didn't need to see her face to know it was Lorelei McCurdy. She's tall and lanky, built just about straight up and down, like a ladder, and wears nice clothes that don't look right on her. Her folks took an awful gamble when they named her after the beautiful maidens who sat on a rock in the middle of the Rhine River enticing bug-eyed boatmen to crash and get robbed. She looked about as much like a Rhine maiden as I do. On the other hand she's as bright as a twenty-dollar gold piece. You can tell that by looking at her eyes, which are dark and deep-set, sort of like Miss Wilson's. Too bad they lived in a face made of straight lines and sharp angles, like a geometry problem.

She was just ladling punch into a cup when Carl whooped, "C'mon, everybody! Grab a partner and —*let's dance!*"

I could see Lorelei stiffen as if a ghost had rattled its chains. Her head turned quickly, far enough so I could see one eye rolling up like a scared horse's. She was looking toward the stairs, the only way out of there. Escape—maybe to hide in the bathroom.

If I could have escaped, myself, I would have, but there was no way. I took a wild look around. Everybody else was paired up. I was trapped. Cagey old Tim, with every move figured out! It would take a real monster to pretend not to notice her and sneak away, leaving her to learn all about humiliation.

I said, "Hi, Lorelei." She jumped and whirled around to face me, wary as a deer in hunting season. I managed some kind of smile and said, "Care to try dancing with a beginner?"

Those eyes searched my face, looking for clues. Was this an unfunny joke? Did I have some hidden motive? Was I just feeling sorry for her? She had time for a dozen other questions but still didn't say anything, so what was my next move? Uncle Art didn't pop up with an answer; Lorelei wasn't his kind of girl. I had to make a stab at it on my own. I said, "Come on, Lorelei! The worst that can happen is I'll tramp on your feet a little."

It worked. She smiled, sort of bravely, I thought, and said, "My feet can take care of themselves, Tim, and . . . and thank you."

She put her punch down untasted and I took her by the elbow (Mother's instructions) and guided her out into the middle of the room where I had to deal with a small panic. This was the real thing now, not my own cozy basement with mother and sister telling me that now I knew how to dance.

No time for panic to get out of hand. From over by the phonograph Carl called out, "Okay, everybody

—we'll start with a *rouser!*" He started the record and here came a tune that everybody knows: "Does the Spearmint lose its flavor on the bedpost overnight?" I found Lorelei's hand up where it was supposed to be, put my other hand on the small of her back, and off we went. *Left*, two, three, four . . . Don't clutch . . . *Feel* the rhythm . . . don't pump . . . Relax . . . Have *fun*.

One thing my mother had forgot to say was "Don't sweat." I'd made it only about halfway around the room when I felt a trickle down my back—and it wasn't hot at all. Nerves.

I was so busy with symptoms and remembering commands—and counting—that the record was about half over when I suddenly sort of woke up and thought, Well, hey—I'm dancing! I'm having fun! Then it took a second or two more to realize that a big reason for all this was Lorelei! She was drifting backwards in front of me, light as mist, and whenever I took a step toward where her foot was, it was gone before I got there. The hand she rested on my shoulder was about as heavy as a whisper. And whenever I thought, *Now it's time to turn a little*, she seemed to be turning already. She was good and I couldn't figure out how she'd got that way. Lessons, I guessed, and a lot of practice at home. Years of it.

I made it to the end of the piece without doing anything disgraceful. I'd already decided it wouldn't do to go sprinting across the room to grab Judy, and something told me it wouldn't be right to drag Lorelei back to the punch bowl and dump her, so I said, "That was fun. Care to try it again?"

Good thing I did because Carl was calling out again: "One more number and then we'll change partners."

After a barely noticeable hesitation Lorelei said bravely, "Thank you, sir, I'd love to try it again."

I said, "You're really a swell dancer."

She smiled and said, "So are you."

That was worth a grin, so I gave her one and said, "You know I can't even talk and dance at the same time. Too busy counting."

The next record started. "Carolina Moon," which I'd heard before, so I knew what to expect. This time I got a little braver about changing directions and speeds. I had to because I was maneuvering to stay close to Judy and Carl. Not easy because I had to keep from being obvious about it. In the process I caught Judy's eye once and she smiled at me over Carl's shoulder.

The smile did it. I missed a beat and stumbled. Not over Lorelei's feet—my own. There I was, a ship without a rudder and no way to get on course again. I don't know how red I turned but I felt like a boiled beet. I babbled. "Oops—too much of that punch!"

The beautiful voice of salvation murmured in my ear. "Just stop a second, Tim; we'll pick up the beat together." I obeyed, and in no time here came the beat, Lorelei faded backwards, and off I went again: One, two-three-four . . . and I said, "Lorelei, you ought to be getting *paid* for this." For a minute there I really loved that girl.

17

The Brass Ring

MAYBE I DIDN'T love Lorelei, but the last thing I wanted now was to hurt her feelings, which could easily have happened if I kept bulling around the floor to stay within reach of Judy. I had a better idea anyway, and it worked. Just kept maneuvering around in the vicinity of the Victrola, so when the music stopped, there I was, about three steps away.

I was helpfully lifting the needle from the record when Carl came loping up with Judy in tow. I could see him sizing up the situation, coming to grips with the fact that his next partner was going to be Lorelei McCurdy. He'd made the rules, so he had to abide by them. I didn't feel sorry for him though; he was in for a nice surprise.

I thanked her for the dances, meaning it honestly, and while Carl called for the change of partners I was already leading Judy out to an open space. I didn't fail to observe that her skin, which looked perfect any old time, was glowing now with the exertion of dancing, and the hair nearest her face was trying to turn from waves back into curls.

Face to face with her like this was as different as beans from bonbons from sitting at a school desk hearing her read poetry. I could not only see the glow, I could feel it. She was giving off heat like a small stove, and it was causing problems with my breathing. No trouble with *her* breathing but she did seem to be having trouble saying what was on her mind. Finally she came out with it. "Tim, that was nice of you— asking Lorelei to dance. It was *thoughtful*."

Now it was my turn to hesitate. It's a lot easier to pay a compliment than to accept one. The best I could do was, "Well, I might have thought I was doing her a favor, but it turned out the other way around. She's a whiz of a dancer, and I'm just a beginner."

I don't know who was calling the signals, but once I'd been so all-fired honest I had to go on and run it into the ground. "It's only fair to tell you," I said. "Lorelei was the first girl I ever danced with besides my sister." This was getting to be like eating peanuts: just one more. "I didn't even *start* learning until Tuesday."

"Well, Lorelei didn't seem to be suffering."

"Not my fault," I said. "I kept *trying* to stomp on her, but she stayed out of reach."

Turning up the voltage on her smile, she glanced toward Carl and the Victrola. "Well, we're about to find out if I can do as well." She stepped up close, holding her arms up, and the music began. Time to start counting again.

My right hand told me Judy's waist felt as different from Lorelei's as if the two of them belonged to different species. My left hand was holding one smaller than mine and as smooth as a canary's wing. Then there was the fact that just by turning my head a little I could catch the scent of her hair. No telling how much of it came out of a bottle and how much was just Judy. Either way, it shoved Uncle Art's cologne clear off the fragrance chart and didn't help slow down my pulse.

I guess girls like Judy learn pretty early how to cool down overheated guys. Sort of like gentling a green colt. Judy's way, apparently, was to bring up a commonplace subject. She tried cars.

"Monday or Tuesday," she said, "my folks are going to get a new car."

I let my feet do the counting long enough to say, "Oh. What kind?"

"Cadillac."

I said, "Wow!" Owning a Cadillac means, of course, that you're rich.

She rattled on. "Dad's wanted one for years but couldn't dream of buying one." I didn't care what she was saying as long as she was saying it to me. "Now, with the stock market shooting up, he says he makes money just by getting out of bed in the morning, and it may be his last chance to get a Caddy."

"What model?" I asked.

She said she didn't know one from another, so now the ball was in my court again. Luckily I had something to contribute. "Funny, but my uncle's going to get a new car next week too. Nothing like a Caddy though. Model-A Ford. Roadster. With a rumble seat. Light blue with yellow trim. Peachy!"

Surprising me, she burst out with, "Oh golly—I

wish that's what we were getting instead of a stuffy old Cadillac!"

I said, "I guess your folks don't think of it that way," and added, "My uncle says he'll teach me to drive as soon as I grow some more. That is, he would if . . ."

I stopped right there, but she hadn't missed it. "If what?"

Her face showed her sudden curiosity and I avoided her eyes. Trouble enough already, trying to keep on the beat and talk at the same time. So I gave her a quick answer. "It's part of this long story you're going to hear on the way home."

She sighed exaggeratedly in my ear. "I'll just have to wait, won't I?"

Since I didn't know where to go from there I guess it was lucky the dance number ended at that point and we had to change partners. There were about ten more dances after that. I didn't get to have any of them with Judy, but I danced with every girl there and I began feeling plenty grateful to my mother. Without her none of this would have happened.

Lorelei, I noticed, kept right on dancing, and I felt good about that too, figuring I'd sort of started the ball rolling for her. Tim Walden, God's gift to the downtrodden.

Eventually Carl's mother and little sister showed up with big trays of little sandwiches and cakes and things, and Mr. Simons brought a gallon jug of mixed juices to replenish the punch, and a big chunk of ice.

We pitched in and made short work of the eatables, and not long after that there were thank-you's and so-longs and see-you-soons and car doors slamming, and finally there was just Judy and me strolling along under the feathery shadows of trees whose leaves were about as old as the skinny little moon that went dodging from silver lining to silver lining while rabbity little clouds sailed along without a care in the world.

April nights can be like that, or they can be dismal and wet and colder than March. I'd already had more luck that night than years of April nights might bring, and now even the weather was doing its bit to make things still easier for me. And what use was I making of all this? I was getting into the story—short version—of Tim Walden and his list of things-that-had-to-be-done-before-it-was-too-late.

I began at the beginning, which already seemed at least a year ago, and my talk with Miss Wilson that led to the list and her advice for me.

Walking along dark quiet streets where Judy's face was mostly a blur was the only way I could have told her all (well, almost all) that had been happening to me since back before Christmas. And in the process I figured out what she'd meant when she said I seemed "different."

I got a glimmering of it when I'd finished telling about Mr. Weinstock and me, and another when I finished the story of the ride-hitching project. But I didn't really nail it down until the Dunk Bolander part. Surprisingly it wasn't the fight itself, which wasn't really a fight but an explosion. The real down-deep satisfaction was in what went before. All those lessons and workouts and all those sparring matches, and battering away at my punching bag, doing everything I could think of to learn how to fight if I had to. And in the process discovering a sport I really enjoyed.

And through all of it finding out I could do things I'd been scared to try. Now I wasn't scared to try. *That's* what was different about me—confidence.

By the time I'd arrived at this conclusion we'd also arrived at the foot of the driveway at Judy's house, which was a big one standing well back from the street, the broad-striped awnings at the front lighted from beneath by lights in the downstairs rooms. We came to a halt automatically.

In all that time Judy had hardly made a sound except for an occasional exclamation, none of which told me much except that I still had her attention. Now, when I stopped she turned to face me inquiringly—or so it seemed in that uncertain light—as if she couldn't believe my overwound clock had finally run down. Then she gave a long sigh, the way a person does who has been concentrating hard for a long time and suddenly is free to stop. In a low voice she said, "And that—that's the end of it?"

I said, "Well . . . well, uh . . ." At that moment the moon did me a big favor by sliding out from under one of those little clouds, shining over my shoulder straight into her face. She was looking at me, sort of wondering, I thought. Wondering what?

Whatever it was, I knew there was nothing I'd ever seen in my life to compare with the way she looked, with that soft light glistening in her eyes.

All that new self-confidence I'd been feeling so good about just seconds ago melted like ice cream in the sun, weakening my knees and leaving me nothing but the courage of desperation. I said, "Well, not quite. There's still this." I leaned forward and kissed her square on the lips.

As kisses go it wasn't much, I guess. Nobody in Hollywood would have paid me five cents to do it in front of a camera. It was strictly amateur night and nobody was clapping. But for me it was the other side of the looking glass and things weren't ever going to be the same again.

For her part, Judy hadn't done anything at all, just stood there. Couldn't have kissed me back if she'd wanted to because I didn't give her time. She was still just standing there and the moon was still doing its job. It was very quiet. Then she said, "I don't get it. What did you mean, 'There's this'?"

Explaining it was about as hard as doing it, but I found some words. "You were on the list," I said. "You were there from the beginning. I've wanted to do that since long before there *was* a list—before I'd ever heard of the end of the world."

She was quiet again for a while, me trying pointlessly to guess what was going on under that gleaming hair. I knew by this time of course that she wasn't going to scream, or slap me, or dash inside and slam the door—any of those things I used to be scared of when I thought about trying to kiss her. But whatever I'd expected, now or back then, it wasn't what happened. All of a sudden she let go one of those bubbly laughs and followed it with, "Good heavens! Whatever took you so long?"

I was spared having to try for an answer to that by the sudden flashing on of the front-porch light. We both jumped and peered toward it to see the screen door open and a head and shoulders appear. "Judy, is that you out there?"

Judy swung around, called, "Sure is, Mom! Tim's

with me. He walked me home from the party."

"Well, tell Tim good night and come into the house. It's *eleven-thirty!*"

Judy called, "Okay—be right in!"

She turned back to me, looking serious, and spoke softly. "I'd like to talk again, about . . . about all this. I couldn't interrupt, but I was thinking all the time . . . and now I know what's different about . . . about *you*: You've always been around and I never noticed you much. Now you're *noticeable.*"

As if that wasn't enough, the next thing that happened was a whisper. "Is my mother still there?"

I took a quick look over her shoulder. "She went inside."

Next thing I knew she'd stepped close, whispered again, "Good night"—and she was kissing me. Judy Felton kissed *me*. The kiss was about as quick as mine was, but it meant ten times as much because it was *her* idea. She whirled and ran into the house.

I don't know how I found the way home, but I must have done it because after a while there I was, walking into the living room to find my father and uncle, Coke bottles beside them, trying to finish a game of chess. Everybody else had gone to bed.

They looked up and my father said, sort of absent-mindedly, "Good time at the party?"

I answered, "Great," found Uncle Art's eye still on me, and couldn't help grinning like a bear trap. "Took your advice," I said. "Grabbed the brass ring."

Grinning back, he gave me a thumbs-up salute. "Good man!" he said.

The same blind instinct that had brought me home told me how to get up to my room and I floated up

there while Judy kept whispering, "You're noticeable—you're noticeable" and a record spun around
inside my head saying, "Yes, sir, she's my baby, no, sir,
I don't mean maybe . . ."

I was sitting in my desk chair, peering vaguely in
front of me, shirt and one shoe off, smiling what had to
be a sickening smile that lasted until all at once it
dawned on me that I was actually looking *at* something. Something real. I was looking at the calendar
tacked up on the wall behind the desk. It said APRIL 19.
Eleven more days now and it would be the first of
May!

CHAPTER

18

Great Day in the Morning

JUST BEFORE SIX o'clock the evening of Saturday, April 30, Uncle Art and I arrived at the little town of Ocheyedan, which is a little to the east of Ocheyedan Mound, the highest point in the whole state, being 1,675 feet high. It's clear up in Osceola County, the northwestern corner of Iowa, just below the Minnesota line and not too far from the Big Sioux River, which is the boundary with South Dakota.

We'd been on the road for nearly eight hours in Uncle Art's brand-new car, covering over two hundred miles on good roads and bad. The good ones were graveled, the rest dirt, which wasn't too bad because in most places it hadn't rained much lately.

Ocheyedan is the kind of town where a passing car is ordinarily something for the old geezers to gawk at from the benches in front of the post office. If you parked a freight car in the middle of Main Street it wouldn't have been much in the way. But—holy cats!—when we pulled into town it looked like downtown Des Moines at rush hour or maybe the middle of

Chicago. First time in history, I'll bet, there were more cars in town than dogs. Cars lined the wide street on both sides, heading into the curbs like cattle in their stalls. And out in the middle was a double row of horse-drawn wagons and buggies, with men and boys fetching water in buckets from the horse trough in front of the general store. Everything on wheels that wasn't parked was rolling up and down looking for a place. Finally Uncle Art drove way north on a side street and found a place. Much farther and we'd have been in Minnesota.

We walked back to Main Street, with Uncle Art complaining that he wouldn't get to see the world's last gasp if he died of starvation tonight. He was just being Uncle Art but it seemed to me an uncomfortable time for joking. Just thinking of what might be in store for us at dawn gave me that ice-in-the-stomach feeling. Nothing new about that and there weren't any pills to cure it. But there were a few remedies that worked pretty well when I remembered to use them.

One was remembering I'd managed to do everything I'd set out to do, so I didn't have a pack of guilts and regrets circling around like hungry wolves waiting for their chance. There was comfort in that. What's more, I'd finished writing it all down—well, most of it—and turned it in to Miss Wilson the day before we left.

Then there was Uncle Art. He'd chosen of his own free will to see me through whatever May Day had in store. There was nobody like him to keep a person's spirits up and lend an ear when needed. For most of my life he'd done more for me than I'd ever done for him, so the least I could do now was to be cheerful when he tried to cheer me, and keep my fears and worries to myself.

One thing more: no matter how hard I tried to forget it, every now and then a picture would flash on in my mind. It showed the compact collection of fishing gear Uncle Art had stowed so neatly in the rumble seat. Even though it went against what I believed, there was comfort in that too.

Now we passed a little park with a bandstand in the middle and a lot of picnic tables, every one of them crowded with people eating the dinner they'd brought from home, and in among the tables were more people eating on tablecloths or newspapers spread out on the grass. Uncle Art said musingly, "The last supper. You'd never think to look at them that they believed they'd never eat another."

I wondered how many really did and how many were just along for the excitement. I'd never know the answer, but anyway, it was a good thing they were provided for, otherwise we'd never have found a place to eat. We got the last table at Sally's Place, which one of the geezers told Uncle Art had the best vittles in town. To the frazzled waitress he said, "Two T-bones and whatever comes with 'em." I stared at him, having seen on the menu that the T-bone dinner cost $1.50.

He grinned and said, "Sky's the limit, sport. You know what they say: 'You can't take it with you.'"

I told my face to grin back, but my brain was busy counting. It was after seven now. Daybreak these days was close to six o'clock. Eleven hours, more or less, and the suspense would be over. When I swallowed I heard my throat click.

At some point along the road that day I'd been

pondering and asked Uncle Art if it bothered him to think of being yanked off to eternity and leaving his swell new car behind. He answered right up. "Doesn't bother me a bit. Tell you why: all I've got invested in this beauty"—he patted the dashboard fondly—"is my old flivver. Borrowed the rest of it. So if the roll is called up yonder the bill collector's going to go right along with the rest of us. In the meanwhile I've had a week or so of pleasure out of it—free, gratis, and for nothing. So you might say I picked the best possible time in the history of the planet to borrow money!"

I thought this over for a mile or two and finally said, "You don't really believe, do you, that this thing is going to happen? You're just taking me because you promised to, months ago."

He took his eyes from the road long enough to throw a quick look my way and boomed out over the chatter of the engine, "Not on your life! I'm doing this for *me*. Maybe I'm not altogether sold on the prophecy—always a chance their calculations could be off by a few hundred years—but I'm a *firm* believer in the fact that your Uncle Art Kenworthy hasn't got an armlock on the truth and never will. So if there even *might* be an upheaval of the firmament at sunup tomorrow I want to be on hand with the faithful."

I thought he'd finished, but not so. He suddenly boomed out again, "Besides"—and here he gave a toot on the horn for emphasis—"Besides, if you think I haven't been busting all this time to take this dreamboat out on the road and *go somewhere*, you better think again!"

The waitress plunked huge thick plates down in front of us, mumbled, "Watchit-it's-hot!" and took off.

I nearly fainted at the aromas that came steaming up into my nose. Besides the sizzling T-bone, there was a baked potato about the size of a guinea pig with a hefty chunk of butter stuck into the slit on the top, a dish of creamed corn on the side and half a head of lettuce with French dressing. We tucked into it as if we'd spent the day on a hay baler and hardly slowed down until we'd accounted for the whole kaboodle plus a wedge of berry pie with ice cream.

Uncle Art gave the waitress a big smile and a fifty-cent tip and said, "Honey, I'm going to dream about that meal, and the girl who served it. That okay by you?"

She turned all pink and sort of ducked her head and smiled a smile that seemed to have more teeth in it than most.

Afterwards he asked around and learned that the great gathering wasn't to be held on top of Ocheyedan Mound as originally planned, one reason being that the only way to get to the top was on foot and a big percentage of the congregation were old enough to be a lot better at praying than climbing. So the deacons or whoever was running things had to settle for a lower hill to the east, over toward Rush Lake. This hill had a name that was almost forgotten now because the locals had taken to calling it Mount Millenium. Anyway, the old-timers said, you could look from the lower hill and see the rising sun, if the weather was good, as it struck the tip of the Mound and signaled the arrival of the fateful day.

Next thing was to get to the place and find a spot to lay our bedrolls out in case we might need to nap a little during the proceedings. We stopped in the drugstore and Uncle Art got instructions from the proprietor on how to proceed, including a place to leave the car, which was a pasture partway up the slope. The farmer who owned it, the druggist said, would charge us twenty-five cents. Uncle Art remarked that the man must be planning to spend his last hours on earth counting money.

"Greed," said the druggist darkly, "is one of the seven deadly sins, as that man will learn to his sorrow."

Uncle Art cast an eye toward the soda fountain. "Those doughnuts," he said. "You giving 'em away?"

The druggist looked like he'd been asked for a pint of blood and started to shake his head but apparently remembered his little preachment, and in about the time a deep breath would take he came up with another. "I am a businessman," he said, "and for thirty years I've run my business in an orderly way. Giving merchandise away is not orderly. I think you will find that orderliness is listed among the virtues."

"How much are they?"

"Nickel apiece."

"Day old, aren't they?"

The druggist wasn't crazy about that remark. He didn't say anything for awhile, probably battling one of the deadly sins. Then he nodded. "Oh, very well—two for a nickel."

"I'll take a dozen, and . . ." I could tell by the glint in his eye that Uncle Art had struck a temptation he couldn't resist. ". . . And put 'em in a sack, will you—in an orderly manner." He winked at me while the man filled the sack, and said, "Hard to believe now, but we might need a snack before morning. All that song and prayer can take it out of a man. Well, let's move. Best we get settled while there's light to do it by."

We hardly needed all those directions. Just got in line and followed the traffic. We found the pasture with no trouble and went in through the gate where the farmer, with a muffin pan full of coins to make change with, was working his deadly sin overtime. More of the same on the other side of the lane where another sinner was scooping in money at fifty cents a car, which allowed the customer to set up a tent and other camping paraphernalia. Business was booming.

We took our bedrolls, doughnuts, and canvas water bag, locked up the dreamboat, and started up the long but easy slope of Mount Millenium. The higher we went the more people there were, a lot of them wearing white robes that looked like nightshirts.

Pretty soon Uncle Art gave me a nudge and we angled off to the right of the trail the crowd was following, and circled around to the east. The new grass of spring was friendly underfoot, the ground mainly free of rocks or gullies to stumble into. After a couple hundred yards or so he stopped. "Good place right here, Tim."

Dark was coming down fast but I could still see the place he meant. Where the east-facing slope levelled out abruptly to create the flat space, it made an almost vertical bank about three feet high.

"Room to bed down," Uncle Art said, "plus a grandstand seat for the sunrise. I figure we're about a hundred feet—little more, maybe—from the top. We can't see the doin's up there, but we can sure as hootin' hear it. This way we get a little privacy, and if there's going to be a heavenly grandiosity breaking loose at daybreak we sure won't miss it by being on the wrong side of a little old hill."

"I wouldn't bet on the privacy," I said. "If we can walk around this way so can other people."

"A few, maybe, but it's not likely they'll stop for a chat."

I said that suited me, so we unrolled our sleeping bags side by side on the tarpaulins they were wrapped in, then sat down with our backs against the slope and made ourselves comfortable.

Now that we were still, the bumble-ation of hundreds—maybe thousands—of voices seemed to swell and fill the air all around as well as above. It was eerie—the sound of a huge crowd of people clacketing away and not a soul to be seen except once in a great while when a couple would hurry by. When they spotted us they'd alter course a little and give us a wide berth. Since we weren't with the crowd I guess they figured there must be something wrong with us.

The stars were out by now and a bright half-moon about a quarter of the way up the sky a little way south of east. Below, the vast blackness of prairie was broken here and there by clusters of light—farmsteads or tiny towns.

Uncle Art crossed his arms behind his head and grunted with what I took to be contentment. "Peaceful spot, if you can pretend the racket is just wind in the trees."

"Hard to do," I said, "seeing as there's hardly four trees to the acre around here."

"Add a few. That's what your imagination's for."

While the stars got brighter and the earth darker we went on trading occasional remarks—mainly about things that didn't matter a lot, avoiding mention of what we thought would happen come morning. After a while Uncle Art fished out a cigar and lighted up and waved the match out, making a fiery pattern of zigzags that lingered at the backs of my eyes long after the flame was gone. He took a couple of puffs and I decided it didn't smell half bad out here with an ocean of clean air to drift off into, and no competition from my father's Idolitas. All the same it took me back in an instant to the smoke-fog in the furnace room the night they gave me the punching bag. A lifetime ago, it seemed.

Maybe right this minute, I thought, my father would be down there puffing away while my uncle did the same thing here. Or maybe because of the nice weather he'd be doing it out on the side verandah, with my mother sitting nearby. She always said she didn't mind the smoke outside because it kept mad dogs and mosquitoes away.

And tomorrow morning?

I remembered what my mother had said the only time we talked about it. "I'll get up and dress and come down here to this kitchen. I'll put the coffee on to boil. I'll slice the bacon and the bread and put the eggs out close to the skillet. I'll fix a pan of oatmeal for Aunt Lizzie and turn the gas down low under it. Then I'll set the breakfast table. *Then* I'll pour myself a cup of coffee and sit down with it and wait for my first customer or—or for whatever else happens." That was my mother. No tears and hand-holding for her.

Before I could head it off I got an ache in my throat as I actually took in the fact that I might have seen the two of them for the last time.

It was about the shortest ache I ever had because in about one minute something altogether unexpected happened: I started getting mad. With the end of everything so near I guess I looked at it straighter than I'd ever looked before and I thought, *Why?* Why did my mother and father have to give up living—them and Uncle Art and Judy Felton and Ed Guthrie and me, and a few million other people all over the world? There was no fairness in it! It didn't make sense! It was wrong—wrong—wrong!

Smack in the middle of that angry yelling inside my head, the endless clatter of voices from the hilltop suddenly died and for a moment or two there was a silence so complete I could hear a dog barking somewhere far off. Then a single voice—a powerful one—rose up. "Good friends—your attention please!"

Another moment of silence, then, *"The Lord is my shepherd, I shall not want . . ."*

He went all the way through the psalm, and I can tell you the hairs on my neck were prickling from start to finish. Even so, I kept hearing faintly the echo of my own unspoken words: ". . . a few million other people all over the world." The echo was lost in the roar that came next as the leader called out again, "'Rock of Ages!' Everybody, now!"

There was a faint sound of music—accordion, I think—and the singing began. All those voices, hundreds and hundreds joining in, quavery at first, then swelling up and up. It was an awesome thunderation of sound that filled the night and seemed to jiggle the already-twinkling stars.

More hymns followed, then the praying, led by the same commanding voice. But by that time the effect on me was dimming as my head filled up with a cluster of new thoughts too dazzling to keep to myself much longer.

When the sound volume of the praying slacked off enough for me to be heard I sat up straight and said, "Uncle Art! What time is it?"

"Time?" he repeated, startled. "Time? You got an appointment somewhere? Well, hang on a second."

It nearly drove me batty, the time he took to answer my question. First he looked at the glowing end of his cigar, taking one last puff, then stubbing it out in the grass beside him, very thoroughly. Then he hunched around to get at the watch pocket in his pants. Fumbled to get his matches, finally lighted one and tilted the watch just so, to catch the light.

"Twenty-two minutes to eleven. Now if there are any more statistics you need . . ."

After a little fast arithmetic I burst out, "Uncle Art!" A little high-pitched, so I toned it down. "There are places in the world where it's May Day already, China maybe, and Russia! It's dawn right now in Europe and places like that, but it's not our turn for six or seven hours yet! How can the world end that way—bit by bit? It can't! It's got to do it all at once or not at all! That's right, isn't it?"

I thought he'd never answer, but finally he did, sort of cautiously, it seemed to me. "Sounds logical."

I scrambled to my feet. Couldn't sit still any longer.

Even though I couldn't see his face very well I faced him. "That means you thought of this a long time ago. You knew this whole thing was crazy!"

He was shaking his head. "Didn't *know* it. *Suspected* it. For all I knew those prophets had figured a way to get around the time problem."

"Well, if you even *thought* of it why didn't you *tell* me? Gee-gods, why'd you let me run around making such a dumb fool of myself?" I wouldn't have believed I could get mad at him, but I was working up to it. I raved on. "Jeez—charging off in all directions—working my tail off in boxing class—worrying like crazy I'd never get around to—"

"Tim." Something in his voice pulled me up short and I shut my mouth. In the same tone he said again, "Tim—think what it's *done* for you! How could I put a stop to a thing like that?"

I let that sink in while another hymn began. "Swing Low, Sweet Chariot" this time. The idea that these months just ending had done a lot for me was nothing new. For one thing, Judy Felton had noticed it. For another, I *felt* different. What I didn't understand was . . .

"How come *you* know what it's done?" I asked.

He was ready for that. "Don't ever go in for crime," he told me, and I knew without seeing his face that he was grinning. "You're as easy to read as a first-grade primer. And remember what your aunt said: a family's a public, not a private, institution. Your family's interested in you, so they pay attention."

That was going to take more thinking-over than I had time for now, I decided, and just then the hymn came to an end. I dropped down beside Uncle Art again, feeling really strange, as if something had come unhinged and I didn't know one direction from another anymore. It wasn't going to be easy to settle down to the way things used to be. Nothing prodding me to get this or that done because pretty soon it would be too late. I'd got in the habit of living under the gun, you might say, and it was going to be hard to change.

After a minute I said, "What do we do now—clear out of here?"

"And go where? Anyway, we came to see the show; why not wait for the curtain to come down?"

"What'll we do all night?"

He shoved a thumb toward the bedrolls. "Same thing we do every night."

"Can you sleep through a prayer meeting?"

"Wouldn't bet against it." He yawned hugely and stretched. "It's been a long day. What about you?"

I listened a few seconds. "Right now it sounds like a lullaby. Guess I could doze off for a while."

He stood up and stretched whatever he'd missed the first time. "Let's go visit one of those latrines we saw on the way up."

On the main trail we met a few white-robed figures on the same errand. They didn't say anything so we didn't either. When we got back we shucked out of everything but our underwear, shivering a little because there was a chill in the air now, and slid into the sleeping bags.

I lay there looking up at the sky, which was a glory of stars now that the moon had paled a little as it slid downhill to the west, listened to the praying, and thought back over the months of effort and worry. Plenty to think about in that direction, but a lot more in the other. There was a future now and it looked like forever. I'd got so I liked having a lot of goals and not much time to reach them. If I picked some new goals to go for now, where would I start?

I thought about that, sort of idly, while the praying went on—rising and falling, rising and falling—until it belonged to the night and the drifting of the moon. Hour after hour I heard it, or so it seemed, but I couldn't have, really, because when I came to I was clear inside the sleeping bag, head and all, and a hand was shaking me. I stuck my head out and had to clamp my eyes shut. The sun was well above the small hill to the east and it looked, as soon as I could stand the light, like another perfect day. I could still hear the pulsating of hundreds of voices, like bubbles in a gigantic bowl of oatmeal, but there was something altogether different about it now. No rhythm, and it wasn't prayer. More like grumbling. A crowd that didn't like the show and wanted its money back.

"Wake up, boy!" Uncle Art was urging. "Wake up. You just slept through the end of the world!"

I mumped and whuffled and grunted myself wider awake and noticed Uncle Art had his pants on, so I slid out of my bag and got into my own. None too soon because right then a couple of grumblers—man and woman—came around the curve of the hill. They passed by, giving us a sour look. Instead of looking like people who'd been spared extermination they looked like they'd been done out of first prize. It was clear they didn't think highly of a man and boy who could stand around shirtless and barefoot in the dewy grass at a time like this, grinning at each other like a couple of pianos.

Once they were out of sight Uncle Art slipped into his shirt, socks, and shoes while I followed suit. "Okay, sport," he said. "Church has let out. Let's head for the lake and catch ourselves a mess of fish!"

We caught a lot, some of them real whoppers, and I enjoyed myself. Still, it didn't give me quite the kick I'd expected. I was beginning to feel sorry for all those people up on the hill. Just like me, they were really going to miss having the end of the world to look forward to.

About the author

During his long and distinguished writing career, William Corbin has published fiction in *Cosmopolitan*, *This Week*, and the *Saturday Evening Post* and written ten other books for young readers. Two of these— *Smoke* and *Horse in the House*—were produced and shown as television series, the first in the United States (Disney World) and the second in England (Thames Television). His most recent novel was *A Dog Worth Stealing*.

Three of Mr. Corbin's books were Junior Literary Guild Selections, and others won awards from the Boys Club of America, the Child Study Association, and the Northwest Library Association.

William Corbin and his wife, Eloise McGraw, also a writer, live in Lake Oswego, Oregon.